AF094015

SNOW WHITE TURNS EBONY BLACK

A Fascinating Tale of Self Transformation

Maimoonah MK

Illustrated by:
Preetha Prakash and Ankit Anil

Chennai • Bangalore

CLEVER FOX PUBLISHING
Chennai, India

Published by CLEVER FOX PUBLISHING 2023
Copyright © Maimoonah MK 2023

All Rights Reserved.
ISBN: 978-93-56482-10-4

This book has been published with all reasonable efforts taken to make the material error-free after the consent of the author. No part of this book shall be used, reproduced in any manner whatsoever without written permission from the author, except in the case of brief quotations embodied in critical articles and reviews.

The Author of this book is solely responsible and liable for its content including but not limited to the views, representations, descriptions, statements, information, opinions and references ["Content"]. The Content of this book shall not constitute or be construed or deemed to reflect the opinion or expression of the Publisher or Editor. Neither the Publisher nor Editor endorse or approve the Content of this book or guarantee the reliability, accuracy or completeness of the Content published herein and do not make any representations or warranties of any kind, express or implied, including but not limited to the implied warranties of merchantability, fitness for a particular purpose. The Publisher and Editor shall not be liable whatsoever for any errors, omissions, whether such errors or omissions result from negligence, accident, or any other cause or claims for loss or damages of any kind, including without limitation, indirect or consequential loss or damage arising out of use, inability to use, or about the reliability, accuracy or sufficiency of the information contained in this book.

CONTENTS

1. Queen Cyprus And Her Obsession 1
2. Lady Helen 5
3. The Queen's Prayer 8
4. Princess Snow White is Born 15
5. Little Snow White, The Curious Child 18
6. Snow White's Obsession 20
7. The Queen's Sudden Decision 23
8. Snow White Leaves the Kingdom of Levon 25
9. Snow White Reaches Cleistra 29
10. The Queen Regrets 36
11. Snow White Returns Home 40
12. The Royal Banquet 43
13. Snow White Meets Prince Solomon 47
14. Prince Solomon Bids Farewell 54
15. Lady Helen's Surprise Adventure 58
16. The Forbidden Dwarves' Forest 60
17. Lady Helen's Evil Plan 63
18. Princess Snow White's Search Begins 66
19. Snow White Meets the Dwarves 69
20. Snow White's Inner Turmoil 75
21. The Search for the Princess Ends 78
22. Prince Solomon Finds Snowwhite's Boots 82
23. The Apple And Madame Quine 87
24. The Disguise 89
25. Snow White is Poisoned 93
26. Snow White is Heartbroken 95
27. Snow White's Melancholy Days 99
28. Prince Solomon Finds Snow White 101
29. HU'S Promise 105

30. The Kingdom of the Whites 107
31. The Crowning Ceremony 120
32. The Dark Kingdom 124
33. Murra 131
34. Snow White Wins the Camel Race 133
35. The Most Beautiful Black Princess 135
36. The Oromo Crown 139
37. Prince Igobo 142
38. Snow White Wins the Oromo Crown 143
39. Queen Hayat's Wish 145
40. The Insight 147
41. Snow White Decides to ask for the Colour Transformation Herb 149
42. Nature's Secret Sanctuary 152
43. The Protectors of the Planet 167
44. The Ritual 171
45. Snow White's Self-Transformation 176
46. Snow White Goes Back to her Kingdom 179
47. Snow White Turns Ebony Black 187
48. Ebony Black and the People of Levon 193
49. Queen Ebony Black 196
50. Queen Ebony Black Wears the Wreath of Holly Oak 203

March 19, 1890

Hello readers,

I am Ebony Black from the Kingdom of Levon. I am going to narrate an inspiring tale of a princess who travelled to three different worlds with her seven dwarf friends. During the course of her journeys, she learns, unlearns and relearns a lot of life lessons. She undergoes a gradual metamorphosis and gets transformed into her beautiful, authentic self. I hope this powerful and inspiring tale of self-exploration and self-realization motivates you to discover, accept and embrace your true self and inspires you to embark on your journey of self-discovery.

*L*et me take you to the Kingdom of Levon some seventy years ago during the year 1820. This vast kingdom was then ruled by a wise and lawful ruler named King Arthur and his beautiful Queen Consort, Cyprus. They lived in a massive and magnificent stone castle along with lords, ladies, vassals, knights and servants. The castle was surrounded by a beautiful landscape of sprawling, lush, green lawns and fine gardens, sparkling fountains and clear, serene lakes. King Arthur loved luxury and comfort and lived an extravagant life with the rest of the royals in his castle. But his beautiful Queen longed for peace and tranquillity and cared less about luxury.

CHAPTER 1

QUEEN CYPRUS AND HER OBSESSION

Queen Cyprus sat on her ebony black armchair admiring her white daisies swaying in the cool, morning breeze in her beautiful garden.

"Martha, isn't it time that you let my little angels out from their cages?" beamed the Queen, her eyes still fixed on her white daisies.

"Yes, most certainly Your Royal Highness. I shall let your pretty, white doves out in the open soon," chuckled Martha. Apart from being the royal housekeeper, Martha was also the Queen's closest confidant and her secret friend though consciously they both never accepted their friendship because of the difference in their social status.

The Queen loved feeding her doves every morning and snipping white blooms from her garden. She was obsessed with the colour white and you could witness her love of white everywhere in and around the castle. Her garden was filled with white blooms of every kind. The castle lakes had room only for white swans and white geese. Even her maids were all pretty-faced and fair-skinned, Martha being the fairest of all.

King Arthur, on the other hand, did not agree with the Queen's aesthetic tastes and instead saw beauty in luxury. He used to spend lavishly on balls and ceremonies, and would frequently hold banquets in the elaborately decorated Great Hall. Swans, whales, roasted lambs and boars were commonly served for the feasts. He would also arrange grand events like horse riding and swordplay and would invite royals from other kingdoms as well. Kingdom of Levon was highly acclaimed for these events and King Arthur took great pride in it.

Life was perfect for the royals of this kingdom. The Queen had everything she desired except a child of her own. But the thought of not having a child did not disturb her more than the thought of having to face someone every day, someone whom she despised the most – Lady Helen.

CHAPTER 2

LADY HELEN

Lady Helen gazed at her jade green eyes in her handheld mirror while reclining on her highly embellished chintz chair. She was considered the most beautiful lady in the kingdom. Her fully bloomed red lips complimented her porcelain white skin and glossy black hair.

"Are my eyes prettier than Lady Ethel's?" asked Lady Helen, peeking at her gallant and courteous husband Lord Ferdinand, who was busy fixing his laced cravat.

Lord Ferdinand turned around to look at his gorgeous wife, "My gorgeous lady! Why do you doubt your own beauty? I presume there's not a soul in this entire kingdom who wouldn't stop by to stare at your enticing beauty."

Lady Helen blushed at her husband's compliment. She rose from her chair and walked elegantly towards a beautifully embellished mirror placed in a corner of her chamber. She met her husband's gaze in the mirror and gave him a coquettish glance, "Stop staring at me like that, Your Grace. I shall not fall prey to your flattery for I only believe the words of my mirror."

She blushed again and stared at herself in the large, spherical shaped looking glass. She parted her ruffled hair softly, tinted her lips in red and puffed her face with white powder.

Lord Ferdinand was still as smitten by his wife's beauty as he was when he first saw her at a ball. "My lady! May I remind you that I was the one who gifted you that exquisite piece of glass which you so dearly love."

"Well, if you would graciously recall as to why you had gifted me this piece of precious glass?" said the Lady with a mischievous wink, "If you have forgotten, I shall remind you that you had pushed away a line of suitors swooning over me to win the heart of the most gorgeous lady in the kingdom."

"Most certainly, my fair lady," replied Lord Ferdinand walking towards his beautiful wife and gently caressing her hair, "I do recall that and perhaps my crafty idea did work in my favour for I won the heart of the most bewitching lady."

Lady Helen chuckled as she always did whenever her husband praised her with words of flattery.

Although she was considered the most beautiful lady in the Kingdom, she lived in constant fear, fear of losing the title of the most beautiful one to someone else. With each passing year, she feared losing her youthful charm and grace. Whenever she was in doubt, she would go over to her mirror and ask, "Mirror, Mirror on the wall, who is the most beautiful one of all?"

The mirror would reply, "You Lady Helen, you are the most beautiful lady of this entire kingdom and there is no other who can equal you in beauty and grace."

And every time her mirror said this, she would laugh and sing, "Well, certainly. I am the most beautiful one of all, the one who has got grace, beauty and brains."

My dear readers, let me tell you something very interesting about Lady Helen. She was earlier famous for something else other than her gorgeous looks. As a young girl, she was a gifted horsewoman, but once the Lord presented her with the magic mirror to win her heart before marriage, she got obsessed with it and her appearance. She would spend hours grooming and staring at herself. And thus, she lost interest in her favourite sport.

CHAPTER 3

THE QUEEN'S PRAYER

Queen Cyprus prayed fervently every day for a child and held frequent congregational prayers in the kingdom for an heir to the throne. The people of the kingdom loved their King and the Queen dearly for their kindness and generosity. And because of their reverence and love, they as well pleaded in front of their Lord to fulfil their King's and Queen's desires.

Finally, after years of earnest pleading, the Lord answered the ardent prayers of the Queen and her people.

Martha was the first to know about Queen Cyprus's pregnancy. She was more than elated. Her joy knew no bounds. She ran to the King's chamber to share the great news with him.

The King, as usual, was having a serious conversation with Lord Ferdinand when Martha interrupted, "Your Majesty, I apologise for this unsummoned intrusion, but I cannot withhold this wonderful message any longer."

The King was astonished to see Martha's presumptuous behaviour for she was known for her poise and politeness.

"Upon my word! What has made you so discourteous, Martha?" asked the King, sounding annoyed.

"My apologies, Your Majesty! My desire to be the first one to share this delightful news with you made me take this ludicrous step," said Martha, feeling ashamed.

"Well, what is that you want to say?" asked King Arthur eagerly.

"Your Majesty! I take this as an honour and privilege to inform you that we are soon to welcome an heir to our kingdom."

The King's countenance immediately changed from a look of surprise to that of delight. Lord Ferdinand was also equally delighted.

"This is indeed great news, Martha," exclaimed Lord Ferdinand, "I shall apprise all the royals about it."

He walked briskly towards the door with Martha following him.

The King invited all the people of his kingdom along with the royals, for the grand announcement. The people gathered in the arena while the royals took their seats in the main gallery. Lady Helen who was seated next to her husband looked ethereal in blue silk.

The Queen very carefully rose from her seat and waved at her people. She started with a prayer of gratitude, "Oh Lord! Thank you for all your blessings and continue blessing the rulers and the people of Levon, Amen. My dear people! I know how fervently you have all been praying for an heir, I do not wish to keep you waiting any longer for I too cannot wait to share this delightful news among you," she paused for a moment to wipe her tears and then continued, "We are soon to welcome a little princess or a prince to our kingdom."

The people of Levon were elated to hear this wonderful news. Their joy knew no bounds. They applauded and cheered with delight, "Long live our Queen! Long Live our King!"

The King was pleased seeing the love and affection of his people for the Queen and their future heir. He commanded his guards to distribute baskets of red, juicy apples to everyone gathered in the arena including the servants of his castle.

"These apples represent our love, gratitude and embracement for all that we have been bestowed by our Lord," said the King, holding an apple in his hand.

Lady Helen took one bright, red apple from the basket placed in front of her. She stared at it. A strange emotion started bubbling within her, distressing her for a moment. She felt uneasy and immediately placed it back in the basket.

Soon after the public announcement ceremony, the Queen was taken to a birthing chamber by her chambermaids. The private chamber was covered with calming tapestries and religious items were scattered everywhere.

Though light from outside was not allowed to enter the birthing chamber, the Queen walked over to a little window and whispered to her housekeeper, "Martha, please bring my favourite ebony chair and place it close to the window and don't forget to bring some white blossoms in my china."

"Your Royal Highness, pardon me for refuting, but I am instructed by the King to cover the windows with thick drapes," said Martha in a nervous whisper.

"Oh, my dear Martha! You know how much I adore the snow flurries; I cannot stop myself from watching them, especially during the dark hours at night," beamed the Queen with a childish twinkle in her eyes, "I am sure the King will understand, do not worry about that."

Martha looked at the Queen with concern and went to get her favourite chair and flowers.

Lady Helen who had escorted the Queen along with the other royal ladies looked at the Queen and gave a wry smile, "Your Royal Highness, I pray that you bear a son as wise and chivalrous as our King."

The Queen paid no heed to Lady Helen's words. She instead strolled towards Martha who had come back with the flowers.

"Martha, do you know why these freshly picked blooms are so mysteriously gorgeous and heavenly?" asked the Queen sarcastically.

Martha very well knew what the Queen was hinting at. She looked at Lady Helen who was clenching her fists in fury.

"Pardon me, Your Royal Highness. I do not know the reason, for I am ignorant on subjects like these," said Martha nervously.

Queen Cyprus sneered at Lady Helen. She would never spare a chance to taunt the lady sarcastically.

"Oh, my dear Martha, you are so naïve. Well, allow me to reveal something beautiful about these breath-taking blossoms," chuckled the Queen, "These blossoms do not expect praises from everyone around, for they are aware of their beauty."

Lady Helen flounced out of the birthing chamber after giving Martha a cold stare. She threw open her chamber door and yelled at her husband, "How dare she insult me in front of the maids?"

"Calm down, dearest. Do not get vexed about the Queen's remarks, I have always told you not to pay heed to them, my beloved," said Lord Ferdinand with a look of deep concern.

Lady Helen glared angrily at her husband. "Pay no heed? I have been enduring her mockery and insidious remarks for long, I shall not take it anymore. What wrong have I done to her? Is it my fault that I am more gorgeous than her?"

Lord Ferdinand sighed and left the chamber as he always did whenever he found his wife in deep distress.

"Whom shall I share my grief with? I have no one to confide my feelings to?" cried Lady Helen as tears streamed down her face.

Back in the birthing chamber, the Queen looked at Martha who gave her a reproving look. Martha felt that the Queen's taunts at the Lady were needless.

"Martha, do you think I was being too spiteful and unkind to the Lady?" asked the Queen with a look of guilt. Martha kept quiet. The Queen got the reply from her silence.

"Forgive me, oh Lord, if I have acted wrong," pleaded the Queen, her eyes closed and hands folded.

She sat in deep contemplation for a long time. After her prayer of forgiveness, she prayed to God to bless her with a princess with skin as white as the soft, supple snowflakes and features more charming than that of Lady Helen.

Martha looked at the Queen and thought to herself, "I wish my Queen had apologised to the Lady instead of asking the Lord for forgiveness."

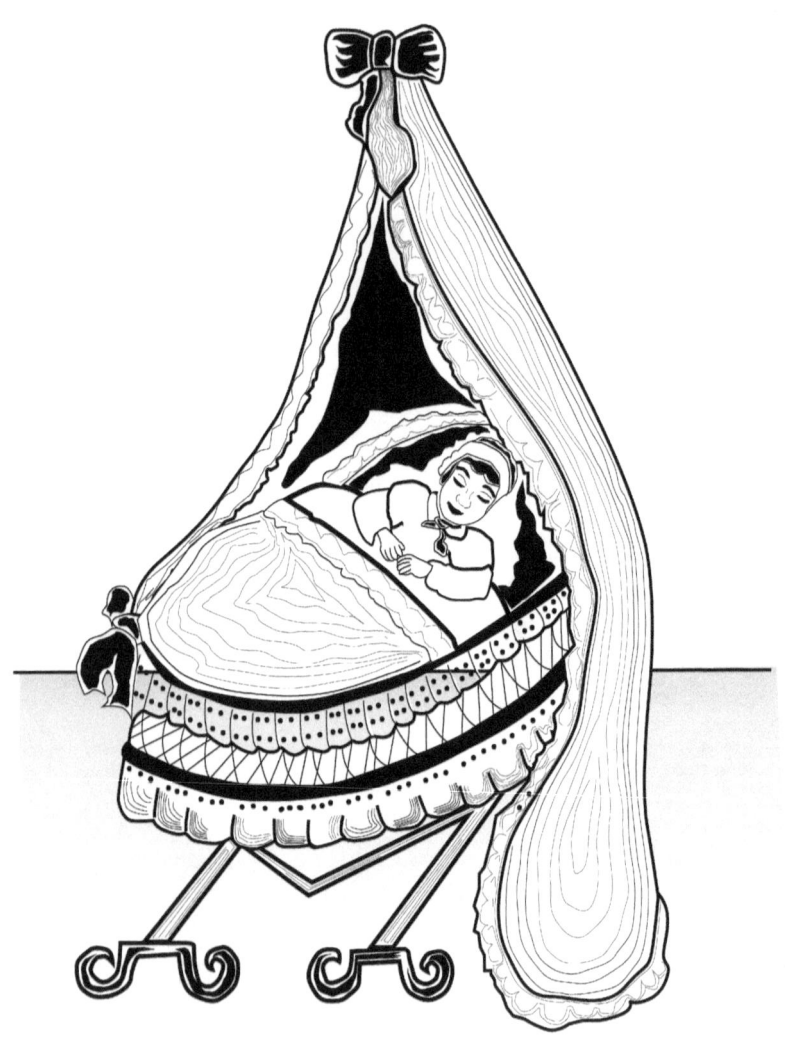

CHAPTER 4

PRINCESS SNOW WHITE IS BORN

The castle was abuzz with sounds of chatter and activities. The whole kingdom was rejoicing and celebrating the arrival of the new-born. King Arthur had arranged a grand feast later at night for celebrating the birth of their child. As soon as the news of the little Princess's pure white skin and ocean blue eyes had reached the ears of the royals in the kingdom, they rushed towards the birthing chamber and thronged inside to get a glimpse of the angelic beauty.

King Arthur's eyes were twinkling with mirth seeing his precious little daughter sleeping peacefully in a royal wooden cradle on red velvet.

Lady Helen, dressed in the perfect silk, walked in at last. Everyone turned their gaze towards the elegant lady with the perfect gait.

The Queen was anguished seeing her and Lady Helen could read that clearly in the Queen's eyes. She ignored the Queen and walked towards the cradle in her usual gait. And very carefully, she took the little Princess in her arms and gasped in awe.

The Queen pursed her lips in displeasure.

Lady Helen brushed off the Queen's spiteful stare and diverted her attention towards the Princess. She kept the baby close to her chest and whispered softly, "Your Royal Highness! Open your beautiful eyes! We can no longer wait to witness their charm."

And to everyone's surprise, the little Princess opened her eyes slowly and yawned.

"Bless my soul! Her eyes can put a glistening diamond to shame," said Lady Helen ecstatically.

Everyone gasped at the icy blue eyes of the Princess. The King looked fondly at his beautiful little daughter.

"Have you decided on a name for our precious little one, Your Grace?" asked the King proudly.

The Queen nodded and looked at her baby fondly. She felt like a proud mother who had acquired a rare treasure. Her treasure was exactly what she had wished for. She was ever grateful to her Lord for fulfilling her wish, for her baby had all those features that she had asked for - she had skin which was as white and pure as the soft snowflakes, her hair was darker than her favourite ebony chair, her lips were like the delicate petals of the pink blossoms in her garden and her eyes were icy blue which no one had ever seen before.

"My Lord, I have decided to name our beautiful daughter Snow White," said the Queen smiling as if satisfied.

"Your Grace, you have indeed chosen the perfect name for our beloved daughter, for she is as beautiful as the soft, supple snowflakes," said the King looking fondly at his wife and daughter.

Lady Helen looked at the Queen who was giving her a cold stare. She put the baby back in the cradle and said in a low voice, "Long live our Princess and may God protect her from every evil."

"Amen," replied the Queen turning her gaze away from the Lady.

CHAPTER 5

LITTLE SNOW WHITE, THE CURIOUS CHILD

Five years had passed. Princess Snow white had now grown into an adorable little girl. She was a sweet and cheerful child who loved playing with her furry friends in the garden and talking to her favourite horse, White Beauty. She was very inquisitive, talkative and had lots of questions to ask on things which were beyond her comprehension.

"Mother, why do people sit on the horse's back and get applauded for doing such a cruel act? Aren't they hurting those poor animals?"

"Mother, why don't all these people who work so hard in the castle sit with us to have their meals?"

"Mother, why do you and father always want someone else to do your chores?"

"Mother, why do you kill and roast those poor swans, whales and boars? How could you not feel guilty eating them?"

These were some of Snow White's baffling questions which made the Queen perplexed and even guilty. Instead of answering them and giving her views on these innocent questions, the Queen would leave them unanswered, for she believed it was wise that Snow White found out the answers herself once she was mature enough to understand. The Queen always wanted her daughter to have her own views and opinions in life. She did not want Snow White to get influenced by the opinions of others.

But Snow White failed to understand her mother and perceived her as cold and passive. She, therefore, started getting closer to Lady Helen who was giving her the affection that she expected from her mother. The Lady's dominant character started influencing Snow white's beliefs and ideas.

The lady would tell her stories of beautiful princesses and the chivalrous princes of faraway kingdoms. She taught her etiquettes a Princess had to follow, how to walk gracefully and speak elegantly.

Slowly the curious and playful little Snow White started showing signs of sophistication and finesse, signs which the Queen thought were too early for a little child to embody.

CHAPTER 6

SNOW WHITE'S OBSESSION

The Queen peered out of her chamber window and was admiring her daughter who was looking gorgeous and elegant in pink silk. Time seemed to speed up after the Princess's birth. She was now a young twelve-year-old.

The admiration and praises Snow White was getting from everyone in the kingdom had made her very conscious of her physical appearance. The Queen was getting worried about Snow White's obsession with her beauty.

"Martha! Do you feel the same as I?" asked the Queen staring at her daughter who was gazing at her own reflection in the lake, "Is my daughter getting too obsessed with her fine features and fair countenance?"

Martha was equally concerned about the Princess who as a child had been affectionate and extremely fond of her. But later, during the Princess's growing years, Lady Helen managed to keep her away from Martha's influence.

"I am afraid I too did notice the great change in her, Your Royal Highness.... But....... But it isn't her fault ......you see it's....

uhm.... I mean," Martha stopped herself from speaking any further.

The Queen looked beadily at Martha for a while and suddenly realized her look was making Martha uncomfortable. "I am sorry, Martha. Your unfinished lines always bother me. But I precisely understood what you tried to convey. In fact, I have been pondering on this same matter for long."

"Pardon me, Your Royal Highness. But I presume it's inappropriate for a servant to tittle tattle," said Martha, looking rather perturbed.

"Martha, do not get apprehensive; I shall not disclose our conversations to anyone in this castle, not even the King," said the Queen in a half-whisper.

Martha shook her head slowly, knelt facing the Queen and said in a hushed voice, "I am not worried about my reputation, Your Royal Highness. I am only concerned about our Princess, I.... I do not wish to cause her...... any trouble, but Your highness, I cannot stop myself from sharing my concerns with you, for I....... I believe you can surely find a solution to help our dear Princess open her eyes to....to reality."

She took a long pause and was finding it difficult to speak. The Queen smiled at Martha, "Go on, Martha. I know you too well and I even know your fondness for my daughter."

Hearing the Queen's assuring words, Martha took the courage to speak what she felt was right, "Your Royal Highness! Princess Snow White shows very little interest to ride on her White Beauty these days and she has not touched her sword for quite some time now."

"Hmm, I do know about this change in my daughter, Martha," sighed Queen Cyprus, "Martha, I am worried......I am worried that she might turn into another Lady Helen, which I so dreadfully fear."

The teary-eyed Queen then squinted at her daughter who was busy talking to the Lady. She knew for sure the person responsible for instigating these beliefs in her. As a responsible mother, Queen Cyprus decided to keep her daughter away from the Lady.

"Martha, it's time that I take the necessary steps to stop my daughter from being influenced any further by that insolent lady."

CHAPTER 7

THE QUEEN'S SUDDEN DECISION

In the days that followed, the Queen spend her time feeling distressed and lost in thoughts. Snow White had completely stopped listening to the Queen and had started spending more time with Lady Helen.

The Lady's frequent advices to her daughter always echoed in the Queen's ears, "Your Highness! Stay away from the Sun, it can harm your clear white skin", "My beautiful doll, you are not taking enough care of your hair either, good heavens, it has lost its silky texture."

Queen Cyprus tried different ways in keeping her daughter away from the Lady, but they all proved ineffective. Finally, one day, the Queen decided to take a major step. She went over to the King to inform him about an important decision she had made.

"What makes you come here so early during the day, Your Grace?" asked the King curiously.

"My Lord! I have something important to announce," the Queen quivered, "My decision might sound grave but I suppose you might comply with me."

The King looked a little perplexed as the Queen had never taken any decision earlier without consulting him.

"I have decided to send our dear daughter to my sister Catherine's castle in……uhm…. Cleistra, to….to stay there for at least ……. four years," the Queen added with tears in her eyes.

The King rose from his chair and glared at the Queen in horror. He was shocked to hear the Queen's sudden and unexpected decision.

"Good Heavens! What on earth has made you take such a grave decision? Can you live without our beloved daughter even for a single day?" groaned the King.

Queen Cyprus started sobbing listening to the King's remarks, "Yes, it is going to be extremely difficult for me but…. but I have taken this decision keeping in mind the wellbeing of our daughter. I want our beloved daughter to be strong and virtuous, she is, after all, the only heir to the throne," cried the Queen. "If she stays here, she shall be influenced by someone else's beliefs and ideas and ….and I…… I do not…. want that to happen to my daughter."

The King knew exactly what his wife meant. He knew his wife's dislike for Lady Helen. "Hmm, alright then," said the King grimly. "If you have taken this decision for our daughter's sake, then let's make arrangements for her departure."

CHAPTER 8

SNOW WHITE LEAVES THE KINGDOM OF LEVON

Snow White was heartbroken hearing her mother's sudden decision.

"How could you, Mother? How could you take such a cruel decision?" bellowed Snow White loudly.

The Queen tried to explain but Snow White had turned deaf ears.

"You are jealous of your own daughter, Mother. Lady Helen is right, you only care about yourself," cried Snow White and ran away, making her mother sob as well.

Snow White trotted over to her father's chamber and saw him having an important discourse with Lord Ferdinand and the ministers.

She dashed inside and did not bother to stop herself from venting, "Father! Did you also agree to mother's wicked plan of sending me away to a place I have no idea about? What crime did I do? How could mother be so cruel to me? She has always been very passive and cold and now she wants me to stay away from her completely. Please, father. Do not send me away. I do not wish to stay in that dilapidated castle."

"My beloved daughter, it's for your own good that we have taken such a decision and this is going to be difficult for us as well," said the King sadly. "Your mother and I do not take any decision in haste." The King was feeling ashamed discussing his personal affairs in front of his ministers.

Lord Ferdinand looked at King Arthur who was in a dilemma. He could sense the King's discomfort.

The Lord strode towards Snow White who was crying miserably. He took her hand in his and whispered softly, "Your Highness! Do not stress yourself. Believe me, His Majesty is known for his righteousness. He shall never take a step which isn't for your own good. He loves you and wishes the best for you because you are the heir to his throne."

Snow White listened quietly to Lord Ferdinand and said nothing. She stood in front of her father for some time sobbing. She knew once her mother had decided on something, there was no turning back and it was futile to argue with her. Her father always complied and gave in to her mother's decisions.

King Arthur felt weak at heart seeing his beloved daughter sob. He walked out from his chamber with Lord Ferdinand following him, leaving his grief-stricken daughter behind.

"I shall never forgive mother for this," cried Snow White and tromped out of her father's chamber crying.

The maids were astonished to see their Princess in an unwomanly manner. They mumbled to each other, "Good heavens! Why does our ever-graceful Princess run so unfashionably?" said one,

"Our Princess had always been so elegant and sophisticated in her manners," whispered another.

They all looked worried seeing their beautiful Princess's sudden inappropriate manners, except for Martha. She was smiling and was happy to see the young Princess cry like how she used to when she was little.

"Why do you worry, dearies? Our Princess can very well cry like other children of her age, can't she?" grinned Martha at the maids. "She's still a child who is living a life of pretence at such a very young age." She then closed her eyes and prayed silently, "May the Lord lead our Princess to the path that she is supposed to tread, for I believe she is no ordinary princess."

The maids gasped at Martha's remarks and looked at each other in surprise. But deep inside they too loved the little, curious girl that their Princess once had been – full of love and joy.

My dear readers.... Let me introduce you to Queen Cyprus's sister, Catherine. Unlike Queen Cyprus, her sister Catherine had no obsession with the colour white, in fact, she saw beauty in the character and mannerisms of people. She even raised her two daughters with the right moral values and not with any unwanted etiquette that the royals usually followed. Will this short acquaintance with her aunt and cousins positively influence Snow White's life? Let's wait and see....

CHAPTER 9

SNOW WHITE REACHES CLEISTRA

Snow White reached Aunt Catherine's castle in Cleistra after a two days' long journey. The old castle was graced with magnificent large trees and natural landscaping. Snow White stepped down gracefully from her carriage and was led by the guards to the Great Hall.

Aunt Catherine was standing at the entrance of the hall with her two daughters. They were beaming with excitement. It had been almost seven years since they had last met her.

Her aunt kissed her affectionately and her cousins gave her a warm embrace.

"Welcome to Cleistra, my lovely niece. I have been dying to see you," said Aunt Catherine with a warm smile, "You indeed have grown into a gorgeous young maiden."

Snow White faked a smile. She looked at her aunt who in no way resembled her mother except for the pale skin and deep blue eyes. Her aunt had thick auburn hair and was a little taller than her mother.

Emma, Snow White's elder cousin, was a few years older than her and was a spitting image of her aunt. And Evelyn, though a year younger than Snow White, looked more like a grown-up toddler. She was a puny, skinny girl with curly brown hair and freckles all over her face. Both her cousins wore lavishly trimmed frocks which looked rather bizarre to Snow White.

Evelyn kept grinning at Snow White while occasionally pinching Emma. Snow White forced a smile at her cousins.

"Your cousins were eagerly waiting to meet you, my dearest," chuckled Aunt Catherine, "that little Evelyn didn't allow her sister to sleep yesterday. She had flooded her sister with questions about you."

Evelyn giggled and pinched Emma again.

"Stop pinching me, Evelyn," cried Emma. "Oh, how ridiculous you are."

"Evelyn, stop hurting your poor sister," said Aunt Catherine with a chuckle. She then moved closer to Snow White and asked softly, "Now tell me, my beautiful niece, how do you find our humble castle? If I'm not wrong, I may recall that you were just five years old when we last met?"

"Yes, Mother. Snow White was five and I was eight then," said Emma recollecting her stay in Levon with Snow White.

"And I was four," yelled Evelyn.

Emma and Aunt Catherine laughed but Snow White found Evelyn's attitude rather undignified and immature. She looked at them and thought to herself, "My cousins are so plain looking. Oh! How am I even related to them?"

Evelyn felt ashamed of yelling so loudly and pranced towards Snow White. She stared at Snow White for a long time like a three-year-old, held her hands and grinned, "Oh I'm delighted to meet you, Snow White, and I cannot wait to practise horse riding and swordplay with you. Perhaps it shall not be boring anymore." She stuck her tongue out at Emma who was glaring at her furiously.

"Oh, really? You little brat!" belched Emma, "Snow White, she doesn't even know how to hold a sword properly even after two years of practise."

"Girls, now don't start your brawls here in front of your cousin," snapped Aunt Catherine, "Snow White, please excuse their petulant behaviour."

But Snow White wasn't even paying any attention to what they were saying and without uttering a word, walked away behind Aunt Catherine to check her room.

Later that afternoon, Snow white was summoned to lunch. She came and sat with everyone in the dining area. Aunt Catherine had made sure that all of Snow White's favourite dishes were spread on the table.

Snow White hastily took a few spoonsful of vegetable soup served to her and without looking at any of her favourite dishes, she rose from her chair and forcing herself into a painful smile, excused herself.

"Upon my word my lovely niece, why are you in a hurry?" Aunt Catherine muttered, sounding a bit disappointed, "You haven't eaten a morsel of food yet. May I help you with some freshly baked cake?"

"Pardon me, Aunt Catherine. But I had my fill," said Snow White, looking away from the cake her aunt was holding.

"Snow White, the butler had spent hours preparing your favourite dishes. Please do have a morsel of each, it shall give some justice for the time and energy he spent in that sweltering kitchen," said Aunt Catherine, taken aback by Snow White's rude attitude.

"Forgive me, Aunt Catherine if I may sound cocky, but I shall make it clear that I have not asked your butler to cook any special dishes for me…... and at the moment I am not in a mood to have any of these," scorned Snow White.

Emma and Evelyn looked at each other and seeing their mother glare at them, they quickly started sipping their soups again.

Aunt Catherine turned her gaze at Snow White and gave her a reproving look, "Hmm…as you wish, but you could at least give your prayer of gratitude after eating?"

"Prayer for what?" Snow White said, looking irked at her aunt's remarks.

Evelyn was about to say something when Aunt Catherine stopped her and said, "Never mind dear, you may leave. If you need anything you may inform Cora who shall be coming over to your room in a while. Cora shall be attending to all your needs from now on."

"Cora is the best," cried Evelyn.

Snow White was the least interested in that matter. She wanted to stay away from her aunt and cousins for the rest of the day. But as soon as she reached her chamber, she heard a faint knock on the door.

She opened the huge oak door and saw a middle-aged lady with short curly hair and very dark skin, smiling at her.

"Good evening, Your Royal Highness. I am Cora, your chambermaid. Is everything fine in your chamber? Do you need anything, Your Highness?"

"I don't think I need any help from you," scowled Snow White, pushing Cora out of her way.

She ran to her aunt and yelled, "How dare you give me a black slave as my maid? I LOATHE DARK SKIN."

Aunt Catherine and her daughters couldn't believe what they heard. Cora was the best maid in their castle and everyone loved her.

"Bless my soul, Snow White. I think you are being rather impertinent now," cried Aunt Catherine. "Cora is the best maid in this castle and she had also taken on as a nanny for your two cousins when they were little."

"I am not Emma or Evelyn, I am Princess Snow White and I disdain dark skin," bawled Snow White at her aunt.

Cora bowed down in shame. Emma and Evelyn ran over to Cora and hugged her.

"Emma, take Cora inside your chamber," said Aunt Catherine, looking ashamed. "Please beg forgiveness from my side."

"Yes, Mother," replied Emma. Holding Cora's hand, she took her away from the dining area.

Evelyn frowned at Snow White and ran behind her sister.

"Snow White, remember one thing. Whatever you give others returns back to you, so be careful what you give them and that includes words you choose to utter," advised Aunt Catherine, sounding very disappointed. "I am sure you are matured enough to understand this."

Snow White felt slighted. She trotted to her room and banged the door loudly behind her.

Aunt Catherine heard the loud bang and thought to herself, "How could Snow White hate someone just because of the colour of their skin? Is this the same girl who once fed a black raven and begged her mother to let her keep one as a pet?"

CHAPTER 10

THE QUEEN REGRETS

Snow White did not come out of her room for the rest of the day and didn't comply with any of Aunt Catherine's comforting words. She sent a message to her father pleading with him to move her back to her castle while narrating the whole incident that had happened a day earlier.

Queen Cyprus felt dismayed by her daughter's attitude and thought of giving up on her dream of watching her daughter grow into a talented and virtuous young lady. She decided to bring her daughter back so as not to cause any more shame to her parenting.

She sat on her ebony chair and stared outside at the white, soft snow and thought to herself, "Where had I gone wrong? How could Snow White yell at her own aunt for giving her a dark-skinned maid?"

She sat there for a long time and thought of discussing the matter with her husband.

She walked aimlessly towards the King's chamber, lost in thoughts. She found the ambience in his chamber quite gloomy and solemn. The King looked upset as well. The Queen wanted to hold back her emotions to not upset him further.

As she turned to trace back her steps and return to her chamber, the King called out, "What brings you here, Your Grace? Have you any important matter to discuss?"

The Queen braved her miseries and spoke in a calm voice, "My Lord! I need your consent in a decision that I am going to take?"

"What is that you want?" asked the King shortly.

"Isn't it proper that we bring our daughter back from Cleistra?" said the Queen in a quivering voice, "I do not want to shame myself anymore. I can……not believe how…. how my little innocent daughter could turn so….so bitter? I never knew Lady….," Queen Cyprus paused and stopped herself from taking Lady Helen's name openly as she knew the King would not approve of it, but even then she continued blaming the Lady indirectly, "I mean, Your grace, I never thought *her* influence could have such a…. such a baneful effect on our daughter."

The King looked at the Queen for a while and then holding her hand, took her near his chamber window, "Yes, Your Grace! I agree completely on…on *her* negative influence on our beloved daughter but we both cannot overlook our faults as well."

King Arthur paused for a moment staring outside from his window which was facing the beautiful garden, "Look at everything in our garden. White doves, white blossoms, white statues, and look at those fair-skinned maids wearing their white aprons, I guess they are running to feed the *white* horses in the stable."

Queen Cyprus had understood what he meant.

"Snow White has perceived beauty through your eyes and you have shown and taught her that only white is beautiful," said the King. "It is not completely the Lady's fault; don't you agree with me on this, Your Grace?" He paused for a moment and added,

"Let her stay in Cleistra where everything is not white, maybe that can make a difference in her perception of beauty."

The Queen was ashamed and felt very guilty. She had never realized that her fondness for the colour white was influencing her daughter's idea of beauty.

She left the King's chamber in shame and walked outside to her garden.

She saw a white dove pecking on seeds near her white daisies. She closed her eyes and confessed, "Lord! I have erred in bringing up my child, forgive me, my Lord. Please help her get back her innocence."

As she opened her eyes, she saw a black raven in place of the white dove.

The Queen, for the first time, looked at the black raven as a creation of God and saw beauty in it. She took a handful of millets and threw them to the black bird.

Back in Cleistra, Snow White was very upset with her father for not consenting to her request of returning home. She spent a few weeks in remorse doing nothing. But after the end of two weeks, her aunt took her into confidence and promised her that if she would do all those things that her parents wanted her to do, she could return to her castle as early as possible.

Emma and Evelyn showed extra kindness to Snow White and never bothered her with frivolous questions. Snow White joined them in their horse riding and swordplay sessions as they wouldn't let her sit alone during the day.

Both Emma and Evelyn would marvel at the way Snow White handled their horses.

"You are exceptional, Snow white. I can never ride with such grace as you do," Emma would confess whenever Snow White took a ride on her horse.

And every time Snow White held the sword, Evelyn would gasp exaggeratingly, "How chivalrously do you hold that beast? I wish someday I could hold him with the same confidence as you."

Snow White never fell prey to her aunt and cousins' flattery. She thought they were trying to win her confidence to make her stay a little longer in their castle.

Though deep inside she felt a sense of connection and love towards her aunt and cousins, she did not want to show her true feelings to them as she thought it would make her mother happy. She kept a distance from them and was unfriendly in her manner, she would only answer their questions only when she deemed fit, or else she would just walk away after her usual curtseying.

Even after two years of her stay in Cleistra, Snow White remained the same. But Aunt Catherine and her cheerful little daughters never for once failed to show love and respect to Snow White.

Snow White at times felt guilty for acting unfriendly but her stubborn nature didn't allow her to change her attitude, for her obsession with her own beauty had blinded her to all the beautiful little things around her. She missed enjoying the little beautiful moments that life was bestowing her with, be it the joy of playing with her sweet cousins, listening to the fascinating fables of her aunt or enjoying adventurous rides in the snow-capped mountains of Cleistra – she felt she could never fit in their company for she thought quite highly of herself.

Her evenings in Cleistra were spent daydreaming about meeting a charming prince who would waste all his time and wealth on her, smitten by her ravishing beauty.

CHAPTER 11

SNOW WHITE RETURNS HOME

Snow White was now sixteen, it had been four long years since she had left her kingdom. King Arthur and Queen Cyprus finally decided to bring back their daughter.

Arrangements were made to welcome her in a ceremonial splendour. The castle was extravagantly decorated with portraits, candle holders and royal tapestries. A grand royal banquet was also arranged to celebrate Snow White's sixteenth birthday. Everyone in the kingdom was waiting eagerly to welcome their princess.

The golden carriage stopped near the castle gates. The doorman opened the door for the Princess to step out. As the Princess stepped down elegantly, everyone and everything around went still.

Her own parents gasped at the beauty of their lovely daughter, "How could anyone look so perfectly elegant and ethereal?" thought the King.

He looked at his wife who was also seen gaping unmindfully at their beautiful daughter. The Queen stared at her daughter's lustrous black hair which was now long and wavy and her large ocean-tinted eyes were shining in the glory of the sun.

Lady Helen was astounded as well. She felt as though she was looking at her own reflection in the mirror.

With an exaggerated gait, she went and gave a peck on the Princess's cheek.

"Your Highness, my beautiful doll! Welcome back," whispered Lady Helen and then turning around to face the rest of the royals she added in an exaggerated voice, "Lo and behold! Doesn't our Princess look ethereal?"

"I missed you a lot, Lady Helen," Snow White beamed hugging the Lady warmly.

Lady Helen kissed her again and turned to look at the Queen who was waiting to greet her daughter.

Snow White walked gracefully towards her father, hugged him and unwillingly walked towards her mother, curtseyed to her and the rest of the royals.

Queen Cyprus felt hurt and offended. She had so longingly waited to feel the warmth of her daughter's skin, to whisper words of love and ask her about the time spent with her sister Catherine and her nieces.

Queen Cyprus and Lady Helen exchanged glances. Lady Helen smirked at her and went to hold Snow White's hand.

Snow White felt the cold slender hand in hers.

"My beautiful doll! Your people are waiting to catch a glimpse of your ethereal beauty," said the Lady in a silvery voice.

Snow White curtseyed and waved at the people who were eagerly waiting to get a sight of their Princess.

They gasped in awe; they couldn't believe their eyes.

"Welcome back, Your Highness! You are indeed ethereal," shouted some.

"There's nothing more beautiful than our Princess in this entire kingdom," shouted another.

A crowd of children bellowed together, "We missed you, Princess Snow White."

Snow White felt proud and important.

Queen Cyprus and King Arthur were also happy to witness their people showering so much love on their child.

Lady Helen suddenly sensed an unusual emotion stir inside her after listening to all the compliments that the Princess was getting from everyone around her. She had never sensed that before. It did not feel good.

She brushed that feeling away. After all, she adored Snow White and loved her like her own child. She could never forget the little hands that held her tightly in fear, the little feet that would run to greet her every morning and the tenderness and warmth of her kisses then.

She felt guilty for the sudden feeling of jealousy that sprang inside her.

She smiled at Snow White and led her inside the castle.

CHAPTER 12

THE ROYAL BANQUET

The Great Hall had been lit up with beautiful candelabrums. All eyes were on Lady Helen who was dressed in an emerald, sack-back silk which she had matched with a seed pearl necklace and an elaborate hair updo topped with a wide trimmed bonnet with a soft pink lining.

Even though the Lady was used to all the attention and praises, she nevertheless waited to hear them from all the royals in the kingdom, for the words of flattery made her feel very special. She dreaded the day when she would be deprived of this special attention, when people would stop praising her beauty and she would be one among the ordinary.

Like every banquet the King organised, this banquet was no different. Lady Helen was as usual the centre of attraction. She was enjoying everyone's attention, sitting on the dais with the other royals, when suddenly all eyes shifted their gaze towards the entrance of the hall.

Lady Helen was outraged at this sudden disregard; she got down from the dais and walked briskly towards the door. She wanted to see who or what was distracting people and taking their eyes away from her.

Who, of course, could it be than the celestial Princess herself?

Princess Snow White walked in, gracefully and consciously, aware of people's reaction on seeing her. Dressed in a red stiffened silk with a loop-up overskirt and off-shoulder neckline, her hat and hairdo matched perfectly with her fine silk. A twisty updo with a few, long, black curls hanging down loose from her elegant hat touching her white, spotless skin.

The whispers and comments from people in the hall were echoing all around the Great Hall. "Bless my soul, she is so fair!"

"She is a celestial goddess straight from Paradise!"

"There is no one to match her in beauty and elegance."

Lady Helen suddenly got the same feeling she had the previous day, but this time it was more intense. She was getting exasperated hearing these remarks that were once used for her.

The Queen turned to see the Lady's expression. Her indignance was clearly visible. The Lady was breathing heavily. She tried to brush it off, but couldn't. She couldn't stop herself from letting that negative emotion grow. She started feeling uneasy and the discomfort she was going through was visible on her face.

Her eyes met the Queen's, but she quickly looked away. To cover up her discomfort, she slowly walked up to Snow White.

"Your Royal Highness! Has a star fallen onto the Kingdom of Levon? Pray! I cannot take my eyes off you, my beautiful doll," hushed the Lady with a forced smile.

"Well, thank you, my Lady. You too look the most beautiful today," said Snow White with a sneer. Lady Helen did not feel good about that comment.

"Why don't we have a competition, my Lady? There are, of course, only two contenders and lots of judges, you see," said

Snow White, pointing at all the people who were staring at her, "but oh dear, I am sorry.... I guess the judges have already given their verdict, haven't they? I mean look at their eyes, isn't the winner clearly visible?"

Lady Helen was flabbergasted. She did not expect Snow White who grew up in her arms, to mock her and compare her beauty with hers. She let the feeling that she so desperately tried to erase PERVADE. She let it rise and grow. She did not stop it from intensifying. She could see everyone staring at the Princess. It was as if she didn't even exist.

She kept her cool, hiding her dark emotions inside and smiled at the Princess, "Your Highness! Of course, you are and shall always be the winner and I am more than delighted to see my beautiful doll being adored by all."

After a short while, the Lady hurried to her chamber and let out an outburst of anger behind closed doors. She felt humiliated.

"How dare Snow White mock me?" cried Lady Helen. "I had loved her all these years like my own child, how could she turn so bitter? I HATE HER! I HATE MYSELF FOR LOVING HER LIKE MY OWN."

She ran to her mirror and screamed, "MIRROR, MIRROR, ON THE WALL, WHO IS THE MOST BEAUTIFUL OF ALL?"

Her mirror replied, "You, Lady Helen, had been the most beautiful one, but now there is no one fairer and more beautiful than Princess Snow White."

Lady Helen was enraged. She couldn't believe what she had just heard. She became hysterical and kept on asking the mirror the same question over and over again. "Who is the most beautiful of all? WHO IS THE MOST BEAUTIFUL OF ALL?"

The mirror stuck to the same reply, "Princess Snow White is the most beautiful of all."

"NO……NO! That's a lie! That can't be true, no one……NO ONE…. can surpass me let alone equal me in beauty and grace. I SHALL NEVER LET THIS HAPPEN."

CHAPTER 13

SNOW WHITE MEETS PRINCE SOLOMON

Lady Helen's hatred for Snow White intensified with time. She despised looking at her and spent sleepless nights thinking of ways to get rid of the Princess from the kingdom. But outside her chamber, she faked more love and concern towards the Princess than ever before.

But Queen Cyprus could not be fooled, for she could well read the Lady's mind. Finally, one day, she mustered enough courage and went over to her daughter to caution her about the Lady.

Snow White was in her chamber staring at herself in the mirror when her mother walked in.

"This is the most unwelcoming intrusion, Mother," said Snow White, giving her mother an unpleasant look.

"My apologies, my dearest. May I have a word with you?" the Queen asked her daughter with a little quiver in her voice.

"What's going on in your head, Mother?" asked Snow White peering anxiously into her mother's face.

"I.....I think you should....stay away from Lady Helen," the Queen said in a low, serious voice. "My dearest, she is not to be trusted."

"You are jealous of the Lady and me, and you envy our friendship," snorted Snow White.

The Queen was deeply hurt by her daughter's irrelevant remarks, but she still tried to persuade her to stay away from the Lady.

"I certainly do not have any problem with your affinity towards the Lady, but I shall want you to comprehend her thoughts and attitudes," advised the Queen. "My dearest, instead of dilly-dallying with her, why don't you start practising horse riding as you used to when you were little?"

The Queen hoped that her daughter would ponder over her words of advice and spend her time productively.

Suddenly the door swung open and Lady Helen walked in.

"My beautiful doll, Her Royal Highness is right. You certainly have to start practising horse riding," said the Lady from behind. "You were really good at that when you were little, my beautiful doll."

The Queen turned around and was astonished to see the Lady smirking at her.

"I presume you were not expecting my sudden visit or I must rather say my sudden intrusion, Your Royal Highness, my deepest apologies," muttered the Lady curtsying to the Queen.

The Queen stared at the Lady in disgust, "It's terribly presumptuous of you to barge inside our chamber without prior consent."

"Mother, you may not concern yourself with my matters," thundered Snow White, walking over to the Lady. "Lady Helen is my friend and I have given her my full permission to step inside my chamber whenever she feels right."

The Queen felt humiliated in front of the Lady. She trotted out of Snow White's chamber with tears coursing down her cheeks.

Lady Helen looked at Snow White triumphantly and slowly kissed her forehead, "My beautiful doll, if you see me as a friend then you shall comply with what I tell you."

"You leave me with no choice but to comply with you," sighed Snow White holding the Lady's hand.

Lady Helen looked at Snow White's white silk and exclaimed in her usual exaggerated tone, "You have such striking taste, Your Highness, and that includes your choice of friends!"

"Most certainly, my gorgeous Lady, I really do," chuckled Snow White.

Lady Helen kissed her goodbye and left her chamber.

In the days that followed, Lady Helen took Snow White for horse riding outside the castle. In the beginning, Snow White was not very keen and was willing to spend time riding her horse to give the Lady company but in a few days from then, she started looking forward to the rides after noticing someone else riding on a fiery steed one day, someone whose gentlemanlike stature and civilities had charmed her on their first meeting itself.

"What an impressive presence he has!" exclaimed Snow White, suddenly unaware of what those words could mean to Lady Helen.

Lady Helen stopped in front of Snow White and raised her eyebrows, "Oh really? My beautiful doll! Did his presence enrapture you?"

Snow White blushed and was quite embarrassed at herself.

Lady Helen turned her steed around and looked at the tall man who was darting on his steed, not aware of the two bewitching beauties glaring at him. "Your Royal Highness! A diamond always requires a closer inspection," remarked Lady Helen and rode swiftly behind the charming horseman.

Snow White was astounded by the Lady's speed on her steed. The young man stopped near the ladies, noticing them for the first time. He gazed at both of them in awe and surprise.

The Lady stopped a little further away from the young man. Snow White stopped her horse next to the Lady's and pretended not to have noticed him.

"Pray my gorgeous Lady, you were unbelievably quick on your steed," said Snow White trying to sound elegant.

"Your Highness! I am an old hand at this sport and beating me in this shall take a lot of effort by anyone," simpered Lady Helen.

"Yes, my friend, I must recall that you had once told me about your win when you were barely eight, if I am not mistaken," said Snow White.

Lady Helen smiled glancing sideways at the young man.

The handsome gentleman listened to their conversation quite intently, rode a little bit closer to them and curtseyed to both. He looked at Lady Helen and spoke in the most dignified manner, "I apologise for this intrusion, but I must say you are an excellent horsewoman and I would love to race with you someday."

"Well, thank you for your most admirable words, but have we met before?" asked Lady Helen with a coquettish smile.

"I apologise once again for not introducing myself," said the man glancing sideways at Snow White, "I am Solomon Scott, the Prince of Briestwistle."

The lady curtseyed and so did Snow White. "I am Helen, wife of Lord Ferdinand and the beautiful young lady with me here is Princess Snow White, daughter of King Arthur and Queen Cyprus."

"It's a great honour to meet you both. I have come here as a delegate to discuss some important matters with His Majesty King Arthur," said Prince Solomon goggling at Snow White's enticing beauty.

Snow White was pretending to ignore his fixed attention on her and kept stroking her horse gently.

"I must say my visit has not gone in vain, Your Ladyship," added the Prince, still staring at Snow White.

"Pray what makes you say that, Your Highness?" asked Lady Helen, exchanging a look with Snow White. Snow White blushed again.

"I find myself in raptures over the Princess's captivating beauty," said the Prince, his eyes still fixed on Snow White.

Snow White could not resist looking at him. Their eyes met and the Prince could not stop himself from exclaiming, "Your Highness, your beauty is indeed incomparable. I had heard a lot about your bewitching beauty but reality has overridden my expectations."

Snow White blushed scarlet and looked at the Lady.

The Lady did not agree with what the Prince had said. Incomparable? She felt quite disturbed and her countenance said it all.

Snow white sensed something was wrong and suddenly the words of her mother started ringing inside her ears.

"Whatever is bothering you, my Lady?" asked Snow White with a queer look of doubt on her face.

"Nothing at all, Your Highness, I was looking at you both," said Lady Helen trying to hide her contempt. She quickly shifted her gaze towards the Prince and exclaimed in the most dramatic way, "The two of you make a captivating pair, a handsome one indeed."

Snow White's face flamed a fiery red. She quickly turned her horse around and muttered coyishly, "My handsome Lady, are you fond of an evening stroll in the garden?"

"My apologies, Your Highness, I have plans of my own to attend," sniggered the Lady.

She saw Snow White riding away slowly without curtsying to the Prince. "My beautiful doll, have you forgotten to bid goodbye to someone who has been enamoured by your beauty?"

Snow White didn't turn back, she was feeling quite bashful and demure.

The Prince rode past the Princess and blocked her way. He stared at Snow White and went very close to her, "Your Highness! I shall meet you in the morning tomorrow."

Snow White was dumbstruck and didn't know what to say. The Prince winked at her and galloped away.

"The Prince is smitten by your beauty, Your Highness, I presume he might be the Prince Charming of your dreams," chortled Lady Helen.

Snow White sniggered and galloped away thinking of her Prince Charming all along.

CHAPTER 14

PRINCE SOLOMON BIDS FAREWELL

Lady Helen chaperoned Snow White to Lowvalley manor the next day. The young Prince was in the fields outside, waiting on his steed.

As soon as he saw the ladies, he trotted on his horse and stopped in front of them, "Good morning, gorgeous ladies," and turning his gaze upwards towards the pale blue morning sky he exclaimed, "What an exquisite morning!"

Snow White looked at Lady Helen and chuckled.

Prince Solomon moved towards Lady Helen and whispered, "This young lady here is a rare treasure, even her chuckle is enchanting."

"I am quite capable of something more, other than just my beautiful looks, Your Highness!" Snow White remarked looking straight into Prince Solomon's eyes.

The Prince was surprised.

"Perhaps we should race to prove what you said," suggested the Prince circling his steed around Snow White.

"Well, most certainly yes, but I would wish the Lady to join us as well," Snow White said bashfully.

Lady Helen was delighted to join them in the race and soon the three were flying away on their horses. Prince Solomon and Snow White couldn't beat the Lady.

"I never thought that a graceful lady like you could be exceptional on her steed," Prince Solomon exclaimed in surprise.

"There was a time when I spend more time on my steed than in front of my mirror," laughed Lady Helen.

"I have never seen such elegance, capacity and taste all in one lady before," said the Prince, looking very impressed.

"That's why I admire her so much," hushed Snow White proudly looking at her friend.

Lady Helen was taken aback by her gesture, "Your Highness, I can never truly understand you; you always amuse me."

The lady held Snow White tightly. For a brief moment, she forgot the secret animosity she had inside her for the Princess.

The young Prince was amazed to see their friendship and love. "Do I stand to have a chance to fit inside your company, my gorgeous ladies?"

Snow White and Lady Helen laughed and rode away.

Soon the three of them started meeting often until one day it was time for Prince Solomon to bid farewell. "I am afraid to say that my business here has concluded and I shall return tomorrow."

Snow White's cheerful countenance suddenly changed to a heartbroken one.

"Do not worry, my fair Princess, I shall return shortly to ask for your hand, for we both are destined for each other," consoled the Prince.

He then talked to her at length about his family, his kingdom and his friends.

Though Snow White was extremely elated to hear the Prince's proposal, she felt awfully distressed on seeing him leave.

Lady Helen tried cheering her up but nothing could help her ease the pain of the Prince's departure. She simply couldn't imagine not being able to meet the man she so dearly loved the next day.

"I am feeling giddy with anticipation to see you as a bride, Your Highness," remarked Lady Helen with an arch smile.

Snow White could hardly utter a word because of the grief she was going through at that moment.

Once they reached the castle, they left their horses near the gates and decided to take a chill in the garden.

Lady Helen kept praising the charming Prince and his upright character, his appearance, especially his fine countenance. Instead of calming Snow White, the Lady made her weep.

"Now my beautiful doll, that's an unbecoming sound of a cry. Do not drop your elegance," the Lady advised.

Snow White wiped her tears and pursed her lips.

"Calm yourself, dearest, and take my arm before you make us late," the Lady whispered softly.

Snow White sighed, "Perhaps I shall recover from this pain tomorrow."

"You certainly shall come out of it, Your Highness. Now make haste," said the Lady.

Snow White spent the rest of her days thinking about her Prince Charming. She confined herself in her chamber dreaming about her extravagant wedding, the gown she would wear, the jewellery that she would match with it, and her wedding veil. She could not wait to witness the spellbound expressions of all the royals in the Kingdom of Briestwistle seeing her for the first time in splendid bridal attire.

CHAPTER 15

LADY HELEN'S SURPRISE ADVENTURE

"It shall be the most talked about wedding, my Lady," cried Snow White moving delicately between her mother's neatly arranged white blossoms.

"Your Highness, I presume you are rather thrilled about your wedding," muttered Lady Helen with a faint smile.

"You embarrass me all the time," said Snow White, blushing.

Lady Helen held Snow White's hand and started walking in the moonlit garden. Snow White had started taking frequent midnight strolls with the Lady in the garden to discuss about her future dreams.

"Your Highness! I cannot believe you are the same young girl who could never compromise on her ten-hour sleep pattern," exclaimed the Lady.

She suddenly noticed a faint light coming through the Queen's chamber window. She pulled Snow White towards the stable at the far end of the garden.

"Good heavens, why have you dragged me here?" Snow White asked rather shocked.

"Her Royal Highness, the Queen is not in bed as yet," whispered the Lady, "I am sure you are aware that your mother despises me for no fault of mine, so please keep our meetups confidential, she shall not withstand your closeness to me."

"I know my friend, mother envies you and she's jealous of our friendship," said Snow White. "Do not worry, I shall never let her or anyone else know about our meetings."

And about a week after that, Snow White reached the country manor. She waited for Lady Helen behind a huge barn. It was mid-afternoon and the scorching sun was glaring down at her back making her sweat profusely. "I hate the Sun," Snow White fretted looking at the lighted sky.

But the only thing that made her stay in the sun for long was her excitement about the surprise adventure that the Lady had planned.

"Good afternoon, Your Royal Highness," called the Lady from behind.

Snow White turned around sitting on her horse's back and smiled, "Good afternoon, my fair Lady. So where are we heading for our secret adventure?"

"Your Highness! I hope you haven't forgotten what I told you earlier," said the Lady in a lively tone. "It's a surprise, my beautiful doll and you shall ask no more. Come on now, let's fly."

Lady Helen spurred her horse and sped, with Snow White trying to catch up with the Lady's speed.

CHAPTER 16

THE FORBIDDEN DWARVES' FOREST

After a two hours' ride, Lady Helen stopped near a huge sycamore tree. She got down from her horse and tied it to the tree.

Snow White got down from her White Beauty and looked around weakly, "Where are we going? What's this place?"

"Your Highness! We are going to explore the Dwarves' Forest. It's right in front of us. Tie your beauty to this tree here and let's explore the mysterious forest," beamed Lady Helen.

"You mean the FORBIDDEN DWARVES' FOREST?" muttered Snow White nervously.

"Precisely yes, Your Royal Highness," replied the Lady.

"Mother had told me a lot of stories about this forest when I was little," cried Snow White. "I still remember she had said it's…it's a dangerous forest and no one dares to even take a step inside."

Snow White started recollecting the story of the dwarves her mother had told her once and how after listening to the strange story, she had prayed to meet the dwarves in real.

"Your Highness, that's why we are going to explore this place. Because it's mysterious," chortled the Lady, "and there's nothing to be afraid of. Don't be surprised hearing this, my beautiful doll, that your friend Lady Helen has visited this place a couple of times."

The Lady then went straight inside the forest and Snow White followed her trying to catch up. The forest was covered with pines, beeches and yews. The air was damp and the woody smell of the trees and the damp moss filled the air. The swarms of insects and murmuration of birds frightened Snow White.

She kept looking around and walked very close to the Lady who was walking deeper and deeper inside the forest. As they reached deep inside the eerie forest, the sky vanished almost completely in between the tall trees.

Snow White was extremely tired and thirsty. She opened her leather water bottle and gulped down some water and slurred, "Where are we going now? I cannot go any further; I am absolutely parched."

"My beautiful doll, we haven't seen anything yet. There's so much to see inside, come on now. You don't want to miss this chance, do you?" said the Lady heavily. She grabbed Snow White's hand and kept walking further inside.

The air echoed the sounds of the rustling of dead leaves under their feet. Snow White could hear the whisper of birds and monkeys chattering from above. Little squirrels were scampering all over the trees.

It was getting darker and darker as they went walking deeper. The monotonous humming of the insects and the incessant warbling of the birds magnified the intensity of the forest.

Snow White suddenly squeaked in horror, "Aaaaargh."

"Bless my soul! What's wrong with you, Snow White? Why are you screaming so childishly?" vented Lady Helen.

Snow White was startled. Lady Helen had never addressed her by her name before.

But now she was in no mood to ponder over this matter, she was more concerned about what was happening around her in that frightening place.

She looked around frantically, "I.... I just heard...... sounds of.........snakes slithering by and....and there's something....... something behind those holly bushes. Let's go back..... I...I don't feel...... safe here. And it's....... it's getting late, mother shall be worried," cried Snow White.

"Stop acting like a toddler and don't shed tears now," bawled Lady Helen. "Let me go and check. You stay right here and don't move an inch until I return."

"I shall come with you," moaned Snow White.

"Now, will you stop sobbing and stay right where you are?" scowled Lady Helen raising her eyebrows.

Snow White was shocked, she had never seen this side of the Lady before.

CHAPTER 17

LADY HELEN'S EVIL PLAN

Lady Helen walked towards the holly and went behind it. She looked at Snow White and could see her squinting from afar. Lady Helen made sure Snow White was doing what she was told. "Good girl didn't move an inch," chuckled Lady Helen to herself. She began to run very swiftly. She ran as fast as her legs could take her. She wanted to get to the edge of the forest and reach the sycamore tree where they had tied their horses as fast as she could.

It was getting even darker now and Snow White started quivering with fear. The echoes of distant howls and growls filled the air.

After waiting for more than an hour, Snow White trudged towards the holly, praying earnestly inside. She kept calling out for Lady Helen, "Lady Helen! Lady Helen! Please come back! Come back!"

But the lady had by now already mounted on her horse after untying the White Beauty and leaving her inside the forest.

Before riding off, she looked straight towards the forest. A wave of relief washed over her, but it was accompanied by a great sense of guilt. She tried hard to erase all the thoughts that were flashing in her mind, but she couldn't. She started reminiscing Snow White's childhood days when the little Princess would cuddle her warmly and lick her cheeks after listening to the stories of haunted castles.

Tears rolled down from her eyes, "Good Heavens! What did I do? How could I be so cruel? NO……. No, I cannot leave the Princess alone there, I shall not let any mishap befall her."

With a heavy heart, she rode back inside the forest.

Snow White started wailing and screaming, not finding the lady anywhere around, "WHERE ARE YOU LADY HELEN? PLEASE-COME-BACK."

She walked past the holly bushes searching for the lady everywhere.

In the far distance of the forest, she could see an enormous red oak tree. A beam of light was flashing on the grass outside the tree. She trotted towards the light, breathing heavily. The echoes of the rasping, harsh screams and shrieks of nocturnal animals made her even more anxious.

She suddenly felt something slither on her left foot. She screamed and jumped. A sudden throbbing pain enveloped her whole body. She felt dizzy and collapsed on the wet ground.

Meanwhile, the lady reached the place where she had left Snow White. She couldn't find her anywhere.

"Princess Snow White! Princess Snow White! Where are you? My beautiful doll, please answer me!" she cried frantically, riding everywhere and looking all around.

She moved deeper inside. She kept calling out the Princess's name but the only sounds she heard were the cacophony of exasperated hoots and howls. She had passed by Snow White without noticing her as she was lying unconscious, her yellow silk camouflaged in dead leaves.

As she rode past the large, red oak tree, she heard the sound of heavy paws and murmurs coming from behind the bushes nearby. She turned around to see, and could not help noticing the silhouettes of two huge wolves padding along.

She was petrified, "Good Heavens, I shall not stay here any longer, they could be dangerous."

She feared dying in the deep, dark forest devoured by some deadly beast. She searched no more for the Princess and rode off, feeling guilty and sick.

CHAPTER 18

PRINCESS SNOW WHITE'S SEARCH BEGINS

Back in the castle, the King was walking frantically inside the Great Hall while the Queen was silently sobbing.

"Your Grace! Do not lament, no harm shall befall our daughter. I am sure she must have lost her way. She has been going around different places on her horse lately, she.... she must have taken a different route," said the King trying to sound calm though not able to hide the quiver in his words.

"It's all my fault. I am the one to blame, my greed of seeing my daughter as a horsewoman has put her at risk," the Queen cried woefully. Martha tried to calm the Queen though she herself was deeply concerned about the Princess.

The King had summoned his knights to search for Snow White as soon as the Queen had vented out her worry. Snow White had been away from the castle for more than eight hours and she had never stayed away for this long.

Lord Ferdinand was sitting on his chair inside his chamber and Lady Helen was quiet and remorseful.

Time was running like never before. The news of the missing Princess reached far and wide. The King deployed more knights and even the ministers escorted them in their search for their Princess.

Prince Solomon came to know about the Princess's disappearance. He immediately set off to find his lady love.

He was terribly upset as he had planned to visit King Arthur to ask for his daughter's hand in marriage. "I cannot believe this, for how could an intelligent young lady like her ever get lost?"

Prince Solomon disguised himself in a knight's armour and rode everywhere in and around the kingdom. He searched for the Princess throughout the night but failed in finding her.

"I shall not give up. I am sure my beautiful Princess is alive," groaned the Prince as he spurred his steed and galloped away calling out the Princess's name non-stop.

In this chapter, Snow White gets rescued by seven strange-looking dwarves - Hu, Aah, Nah, Dah, Wah, Khaa and Ha. Let me briefly describe them so that you may know them better. Hu is the leader of the dwarves; he is calm, patient and very assertive. Aah is a very curious dwarf who finds everything amusing, Nah is a silent observer and talks very less, Dah on the other hand is very loud and talkative. While Wah is an emotional dwarf and cries very easily, Ha is a funny one who giggles at everything and doesn't take anything seriously. Well, there is one more dwarf – Khaa, the monstrous-looking dwarf who is always angry and hates humans.

CHAPTER 19

SNOW WHITE MEETS THE DWARVES

Snow White opened her eyes and was thunderstruck. She couldn't believe her eyes. She screamed at the top of her voice, "WHO – WHO – ARE – YOU ALL? HELP! HELP! LET… ME…… GO."

Seven mysterious-looking grey men who resembled short tree stumps were peering at her. They had sharp, penetrating eyes, and long, pointed ears and their faces had a texture of old tree barks. They wore tunics made of brown and orange leaves.

"Calm down, we shall not harm you," said a friendly and kind-looking dwarf.

"You may call us by whatever name you like, dwarves, pixies or trees," giggled a funny-looking dwarf with an unusually funny countenance.

"What is in a name?" muttered a vibrant and loud one, "We are born with a meaning and not a name. If we are given a name, it should define us and humans fancy naming their children with the most bizarre names and—"

"That's enough. Do not scare the girl for she's already frightened seeing us," said a calm and serious-looking dwarf who looked a little older than the rest.

Snow White couldn't believe her ears and eyes. For a second, she thought she was dreaming. The stories she had heard about the dwarves were all true. She kept staring at them.

The funny-looking dwarf kept giggling, "Look at her face, she's frozen. Ha... Ha... Ha... WE ARE MONSTERS, WE SHALL DEVOUR YOU UP." He advanced closer and closer towards her making awful, monstrous expressions. The serious-looking dwarf once again came to her rescue and pulled him away from her.

"Oh, my poor girl!" wept a sad-looking one, "Please don't be frightened, Good heavens, look at you. Oh please don't get scared, we won't harm you."

"Why do you shed tears for these destructive humans?" growled a dwarf who looked rather fierce and monstrous. "I am sure she must have come to destroy this forest." He jumped closer to Snow White and roared, "We have been living peacefully for a long time here, STAY AWAY FROM THIS FOREST."

Snow White shrieked in fear.

"OH NO! Hu, tell him to stop frightening the poor girl," cried the friendly-looking dwarf.

The older dwarf who seemed to be their leader stared at the furious one for some time. He walked towards Snow White and said in a deep voice, "My precious child, you are safe here, do not get frightened. I feel you should know us better to get rid of your apprehensions."

He gestured at a dwarf who was standing very still without uttering a word.

"I. Am. Nah," said the dwarf shortly pausing after every word. He placed his palm on Snow White's head for some time. Snow White felt better.

"I am Dah and he is Hu, our master," said the talkative and loud dwarf, pointing to the older dwarf. He introduced all the dwarves to Snow White and even described them in detail.

"Now my friend, you shall tell us about yourself, we would like to know more about you," asked the curious dwarf Aah.

Snow White riveted her eyes on Hu and thought, "Their master has no fine robes and looks just like the rest of them." She scrutinized each one of the dwarves.

"We are waiting," said Aah, again eager to know more about Snow White.

"I am ……Snow White and I am……. a……. Princess," quivered Snow White.

"I KNEW IT," bawled Khaa. "Her father the King must have sent her to capture this forest and DESTROY the foliage here."

"NO! NO! He ……. he didn't send me…… here. My…….my poor father doesn't even know that I am here," cried Snow White loudly.

"WE DO NOT TRUST YOU," yelled Khaa. "YOU ARE AFTER ALL—"

"Stop, you beast," Wah cried. "You shall not scare this poor girl. Hu, please stop Khaa."

Hu stared at Khaa intensely, "Khaa you do not know the whole story."

Khaa gazed away with a grimace.

Hu turned to Snow White and smiled, "Tell us, my precious child, how did you reach this Forbidden Forest?"

Snow White told them the whole story. She sobbed, thinking of Lady Helen, "Poor Lady Helen! I hope she is not in any danger."

Nah walked very slowly towards Snow White. He sat close to her, shut his eyes and uttered his name loudly with a slow breath- NAAAAH. He then opened his eyes, and held her face in his hands, forcing her to look straight into his sharp, mysterious eyes.

Snow White froze. All of a sudden, his eyeballs vanished out of sight and instead flashed something strange. Snow White stared intently at the two figures in his eyes. She was stunned. It was Lady Helen with her in the forest ground before she went missing. Flashbacks of the previous day in the forest were being replayed in his eyes.

She looked at the whole scene and thought to herself, "Why is he taking me back in time?"

Suddenly she saw something bizarre, something which was difficult for her to comprehend. Lady Helen was moving away from her towards the clearing outside the forest. She saw the Lady ride away on her horse leaving her behind. But soon after, the Lady stopped and returned to take her back. Snow White saw the lady leave the forest again, looking very frightened.

She also saw what happened after the Lady returned to the castle. The Lady kept quiet about Snow White's disappearance and she saw her go straight into her chamber. She could see her mother weeping incessantly and continuously inquiring about her from everyone in the kingdom. She also saw her father summoning all the knights to search for her.

Snow white quickly moved her eyes away from Nah unable to watch any further. She was heartbroken.

Snow White sobbed, she couldn't believe what she had seen. "How.... could.... she ....do......this....to....me?" she cried. "I never......ever......suspected her......even when my ......my poor mother.... had admonished me. She could......have .... at least told them where I was.... lost."

She sobbed bitterly for a long time. Wah ran over to her, hugged her tightly and sobbed with her. Ha kept giggling and Khaa, on the other hand, was fuming with rage.

"Let her cry until she comes out of that pain," said Hu to Wah. "Keep talking to her."

"Yes, Hu," quavered Wah who was also weeping uncontrollably.

Hu gestured everyone to follow him, leaving the grieving Snow White with the weeping Wah and giggling Ha.

CHAPTER 20

SNOW WHITE'S INNER TURMOIL

After a two days' tedious search, Prince Solomon found Snow White's scarf and White Beauty in the middle of the forest. He handed them to the Knight Commander who was leading the knights in the search. Prince Solomon maintained silence lest his identity should be revealed to everyone in the Kingdom of Levon.

The Queen cried bitterly seeing her daughter's scarf, but she was now completely convinced that she was alive. She kept praying earnestly day and night for her daughter's safe return.

Meanwhile back in the Dwarves' Forest, Snow White felt a little better the next day.

She looked around the tiny, hollow-shaped room. It was cosy and neat. The walls were pale yellow and had a tree bark texture. There was a little, circular window with white drapes covering them. A stool and a table made of coir were placed in a corner. The coir cot she was lying on was quite small but even then, she had slept comfortably on it.

She slowly got up from her cot and stepped out of the room she was in. She was amazed to see the whole cottage. She sniffed the air around. It had a woody fragrance.

There was a spiral staircase with seven floors in total with one room on each floor. The ground floor had a small living space with a table and seven chairs. There was a small kitchen and a spacious bathroom on either side of the living room.

She wanted to step out to see what was outside, but the door was locked and the dwarves were not to be seen anywhere around.

She huddled on the coir mat and started thinking of her whole journey, "Why did the Lady do this to me? Why does she hate me? Why didn't I listen to my mother? My poor mother." She started weeping bitterly, thinking of everything that had happened to her in the forest.

Suddenly the door pushed open and the seven dwarves stepped in one by one uttering the word 'Peace.'

They saw a teary-eyed Snow White crouched in the corner of their living room, weeping.

A crying Wah ran over to her. Ha started roaring with laughter seeing them both cry.

"Young girl, please sit on this stool," said Aah looking concerned, "Now tell us what happened, what made you weep?"

"I want to go back to my mother," Snow White cried weakly. "Can you help me get back to my castle?"

"Yes, once you are perfectly fine, we shall find a way to get you back home," said Hu. He turned to look at Khaa who was muttering angrily. He gestured him to stop.

Dah walked to the table and checked the meal he had kept for Snow White before leaving for work, "Good gracious! My friend, you haven't had a morsel of food today, aren't you hungry?"

Snow White was not listening. She was lying on Wah's lap and weeping.

Dah took the meal inside the kitchen and came back with a bowl of warm broth, "Now, you shall have this broth, my friend."

Wah took it from him and asked Snow White to repeat a prayer of 'Grace' after him. Snow White couldn't pray.

"Are you not used to praying before having your meals?" inquired Aah.

"Oh, how ungrateful these humans are!" Khaa roared loudly. Snow White shuddered and stopped crying. She repeated the prayer in a quivering voice.

"You scared her again, you angry beast," said Wah giving a reproving look to Khaa. "Ignore him, my poor girl. Now open your mouth, allow me to feed you the broth before it gets cold."

A deep sense of nostalgia suddenly pervaded her whole being. She reminisced her childhood days when Martha used to feed her narrating tales of joy and love. Wah had the same warmth as Martha.

"Oh! How could I have ignored her after growing up?" thought Snow White to herself. "She had been so loving and caring. Oh, how could I have been so blind?" Tears trickled down her cheeks thinking of Martha and her mother. She wanted to hug them both and feel their warmth and love again.

CHAPTER 21

THE SEARCH FOR THE PRINCESS ENDS

The King had decided to end the search for the Princess after three weeks' intense search. With a heavy heart, he called the knights back to the kingdom.

The Queen had become very quiet and remorseful. She spent her days inside her chamber, praying and sobbing silently. She still had hopes that her daughter was alive and would return to the kingdom one day, "My Lord! I know my daughter is alive, keep her safe wherever she is." At the end of this daily prayer, she would feed the white doves and the black ravens alike.

Back in the Forbidden Forest, Snow White was still not completely out of her trauma. She would see snakes slithering and crawling all around in her dreams. The pain Lady Helen caused her and her own disdainful attitude towards her mother added to her agony. She simply couldn't get over it. This made her physically weak.

"My precious child, you have to accept all that has happened to you," advised Hu giving her a broth of fresh herbs. "You have to take everything in a positive spirit and forgive yourself and the Lady."

Snow White tried to conceal her pain and faked happiness outside. But the dwarves could well read her mind and heart. To help her come out of her agonies, Hu instructed Wah, Aah, Dah and Ha to take her outside their cottage, for the first time.

Snow White gasped when she stepped out of the dwarves' house, "Upon my word! Was I inside this oak tree all these days?"

"Isn't it strange, Snow White? This always amuses me, for how could we all fit inside a tree together," said Aah scratching his head.

"It is no ordinary tree, my friend. It is a great healer and has healed many," muttered Dah. "The forest dwellers occasionally come here to sit under it. But do not get frightened if you hear whispers or murmurs during the early hours of the day it's just—"

"Now, let the poor girl alone," interrupted Wah. "Let's have some fun, my friend, play, sing and dance......for these things can help you overcome your pain."

Wah and Ha took her to the top of the hill just behind their home. They both danced and sang wildly, making Snow White smile a little.

Snow White suddenly spotted a red deer peering at her. She chased and caught it.

"So, you have exemplary skills at chasing, haven't you?" Aah asked thoughtfully.

Snow White sensed he was aiming at something else which she didn't quite understand.

"That's Guzza," chuckled Ha, stroking the deer gently. Snow White hugged it and felt its warmth.

Ha started laughing loudly and Guzza imitated him. Snow White found it very amusing, she too laughed with them. Wah got suddenly emotional seeing Snow White laugh. He started sobbing. Guzza prodded over to him and sobbed just the way he did. Snow White was even more amused this time, "Oh, how clever she is. She can imitate everyone."

"She can feel our emotions like every other animal," giggled Ha.

Wah and Ha played with Guzza, climbed trees, and ran behind butterflies. Snow White took some time in joining the fun as her etiquettes weren't allowing her to. But in a few days, she started enjoying the play, she even started singing her own songs and dancing wildly to her funny tunes. Wah taught her to climb trees and Ha taught her the songs of the birds. But her favourite part of all mornings was her time with Guzza, her pet.

"Isn't she adorable?" cried Snow White one morning before the dwarves left for work, "I shall take her along when I return home."

"That we shall see. You have to recover completely before you head back to your castle," said Hu. "Till then enjoy your stay here."

Khaa wasn't happy hearing that. He scorned at Snow White.

"Ignore him. He is always angry," laughed Ha.

Snow White slowly started feeling comfortable and happy with her dwarf friends. She couldn't wait to wake up and run outdoors early during the day. Her friends would wake up very early to perform some rituals, but Snow White would only rise once the breakfast was ready.

The dwarves never forced her or even cared to teach her their rituals or prayers. But she had learnt one prayer – the Grace, and now she knew what it meant.

After the dwarves left for work, she wasn't allowed to step outside the house. She would spend the rest of the day cleaning, cooking, sewing or painting. These were the things she never thought she would ever do as a princess. She enjoyed and loved doing them now.

CHAPTER 22

PRINCE SOLOMON FINDS SNOWWHITE'S BOOTS

Lady Helen kept the letter hidden inside her wardrobe after reading it and then headed straight out of her chamber. She stealthily walked down the flight of stairs and bolted out of the castle. She mounted her steed and rode off without informing anyone.

Her heart was beating heavily, "Good gracious, whatever the matter can be?"

She reached Lowvalley Manor and looked around.

He was on time, looking dashing as always.

"Good day, my Ladyship," greeted Prince Solomon enthusiastically.

"Good day to you, Your Highness," said the Lady. "What brings you here so early during the day?"

Prince Solomon got down from his brown steed and joined the Lady towards the barn.

"My sincere apologies for calling you out during this hour of the day," said the Prince. "But I cannot withhold myself any longer with my very recent finding."

"Pray, what have you found, Your Highness?" cried the lady nervously.

The Prince's countenance brightened as he spoke, "However deluded it may sound to you but I believe that my lady love is very much alive."

But the Lady's countenance conveyed fear instead of happiness and she couldn't hide her feelings, "I understand what you are going through, Your Highness. But I am afraid she is—"

Before she could finish, the Prince bellowed, "Heaven forbid that something bad should ever befall my beautiful Princess. She is very much alive, my Ladyship and I have found something that shall prove she is taken hostage by someone in the Forbidden Forest."

The lady's hands trembled and she was perspiring heavily.

"After the Princess went missing, I would visit the forest every week hoping to get a trace of my love," breathed the Prince. "Three days ago as I was trotting on my horse, I saw a gleam of light in the dark, close to a big, red oak tree. I went closer and looked around the tree but nothing was visible in the dark," he paused for a moment and then continued, "I walked on top of the hill behind the tree and to my astonishment, I saw a pair of brown leather boots which I can for sure say belongs to the Princess."

Lady Helen gasped, she didn't know what to say or think. She panicked and Prince Solomon could not help but ask her the cause of her agony.

"Upon my word Lady Helen, what makes you so nervous?" the Prince asked, staring at the Lady.

Lady Helen altered her manner and cried, "Oh my poor girl, how frightened she must have been alone in that forest, for her etiquettes had never made her walk barefoot when she was in the kingdom."

She started sobbing for real, imagining the worst.

"My sincere apologies to have put you in such agony, but allow me to continue," said the Prince. "The boots were clean and were placed carefully on a stone slab. I believe they cannot stay perfectly clean in a damp forest for this long, can they, my Ladyship?"

The lady kept silent for a moment and did not retaliate for the fear of sounding faulty.

"Your Highness, that does sound probable for our Princess to be still alive in that forest," said the Lady simmering with fear inside. "I shall myself go there and find out, for if I find her, I shall bring her back to the castle."

"I shall chaperone, Lady Helen," said the Prince quickly.

"No, that shall not be required, Your Highness, for our King and Queen are ignorant about your deep affection for their daughter and it may deem improper for them to know during such an unfortunate time," said the Lady nervously. "I shall set off alone tomorrow itself."

The Prince agreed though reluctantly and they soon parted ways.

The Lady rode away, lost in deep thoughts.

"If what the Prince said was true, then Snow White must definitely be alive. Before he takes matters into his own hands, I have to be quick on my feet and do something hastily," said the Lady to herself.

CHAPTER 23

THE APPLE AND MADAME QUINE

Lady Helen prodded hastily towards the Forbidden Forest but instead of getting deep inside, she galloped on a rising ground to the left side of the clearing and from there she reached the middle of woody hills. She rode for some time until she reached a grove which was lined with apple trees. Red, shiny apples were glistening in the afternoon sun.

She got down from her horse and walked straight through a narrow path. An old, dilapidated wooden cottage stood at the far end, covered with moss.

Lady Helen stood there for a minute and hesitated to knock on the door, "This is madness, what am I doing?" she thought. "But……but I cannot……. I shall not let my life get ruined. My husband shall never forgive me if he comes to know the truth."

With an aching heart, she knocked on the door. The hinges of the mahogany door squeaked loudly as someone slowly opened the door.

A short and frail old woman with a long, crooked nose peered at her sharply.

"Good day Madame Quine, I am Lady He………Lady Harriet," fumbled the Lady.

"I do not care what your name is and if you wish to hide you may," Madame Quine scowled. "Tell me young lady, what is the point of your visit?"

Lady Helen told her what she required from her, but she did not disclose Snow White's name or whereabouts.

"Now you shall tell me, the one thing that the girl's mother obsesses about?" grinned Madame Quine mischievously.

Lady Helen did not have to think long. "THE COLOUR WHITE," she yelled.

"And what about the Prince? What does he most adore in the Princess?" Madame Quine asked squinting at the Lady.

Lady Helen had to think hard, she recalled all the words of adulation he had used to flatter the Princess. Yes, she had got the answer—it was the Princess's skin.

"So, he admires the colour of her skin just like her mother," chortled Madame Quine.

Madame Quine thought for some time and after a while asked the Lady to get the best apple from her grove.

Lady Helen did as she was told but with a feeling of guilt and fear.

The old lady collected herbs from her garden and taking the apple from Lady Helen, went inside to prepare the potion. Lady Helen waited outside anxiously. She was feeling guilty, frightened and ashamed.

CHAPTER 24

THE DISGUISE

It was a late Sunday afternoon. Snow White had sat down to knit some woolly hats for her dwarf friends for winter. She couldn't wait to surprise them.

She gazed at Khaa's knitted hat and shrugged, "I hope it shall fit him perfectly."

She was suddenly startled by a faint knock at the window, "Who can it be? Oh well, it has got to be my naughty friend Guzza." She chuckled to herself and opened the small window.

"Oh!" cried Snow White, surprised to see an old woman clad in a long black hoodie, coughing profusely. She was holding a basket of red apples in her right hand.

"Who are you? And…and how did you reach this place?" asked Snow White staring at the old woman. "No one ever comes here, it's the Forbidden Forest."

"I…I am coming from a village nearby," said the old woman weakly. "I had heard about the juicy, red apples in this part of the forest and thought of trying my luck in finding them. I did pluck a few but soon after my mouth was parched and I felt weak."

"But how did you know there's a house inside this tree? No one can ever trace it," asked Snow White curiously.

"Oh well, Mr. Giggles and Mr. Chatty showed me this house," chuckled the old lady.

"Mr. Giggles and Mr. Chatty?" asked Snow White, looking confused.

"How did they look?" asked Snow White suspiciously.

"My dear, they looked like forest dwellers," said the lady quickly.

"Did they look strange…..uhm….like trees, didn't you get frightened?" quivered Snow White.

"Trees?" cried the old lady, "Pray what makes you say that? Those men were just ordinary-looking men but very short. They did act quite weird and so were their names."

"I am sorry for asking you all this," said Snow White warmly. "Well, let me get you a cup of water."

Snow White went inside and hurried back to give a cup of water to the old woman.

The old woman gulped down the warm liquid, squinted at Snow White for some time and whispered, "Thank you, my lovely child." She very slowly pulled a very red, shining apple from her basket and offered it to Snow White, "Please accept this apple as a token of love for your kindness, my dear child."

At first Snow White hesitated, "My sincere apologies, I cannot accept the fruit."

"My child, I presume you do not trust me, what harm can an old woman like me cause you?" cried the old woman.

"Do not lament, I shall take it," said Snow White taking the apple from the lady.

As soon as the old lady left, Snow White bit into the red, juicy fruit.

"It's delicious," chuckled Snow White.

But no sooner had she swallowed it, she felt dizzy and nauseous. Her skin started to itch, and her eyes, ears and nose began to swell. She moaned and groaned in pain and suddenly collapsed on the floor.

The old lady reached the forest edge and mounted her steed. She thought about Snow White and sobbed, "I am sorry my beautiful doll, but I had to do it. I cannot let Prince Solomon find you."

Lady Helen quickly rode away before anyone would notice.

CHAPTER 25

SNOW WHITE IS POISONED

Wah let out a loud piercing shriek seeing Snow White lying unconscious on the floor. The other dwarves ran quickly inside hearing his shriek.

Snow white's face and body were fully swollen. Her skin had turned scarlet and she wasn't breathing.

Hu exchanged glances with Ha and Dah. Nah nodded at them as if trying to gesture something.

"Stop crying, Wah. Go get the herbs," said Hu shortly. Nah placed his right palm on her head and kept chanting silently.

Khaa and Wah ran outside and came back with plenty of herbs. They spread them one by one on a coir mat. The dwarves together lifted her and placed her on the leaves.

"Look at her, I cannot bear to see her lying down like this, why has she done this to herself? My poor girl," cried Wah.

"Enough Wah, keep silent and Ha, you shall stop giggling," said Aah patting Snow White's forehead.

"Let's rub this paste all over her body and Nah, pour this water little by little into her mouth," ordered Hu.

The furious dwarf Khaa was grumbling continuously, "saphead!"

"Hold back your emotions everyone. You shall all now work and pray, all of you together, silently," ordered Hu looking at everyone one by one.

Tears trickled down from Wah's cheeks as he prayed earnestly for his friend.

Ha giggled and prayed while Khaa grumbled in his prayers.

Nah poured the liquid silently and intensely, not uttering a word.

CHAPTER 26

SNOW WHITE IS HEARTBROKEN

Snow White opened her eyes the next morning. She heard soft murmurs coming from all around her; chants and prayers in a language she had never heard before.

The dwarves stopped the chants, seeing Snow White fully awake.

Wah and Ha started dancing and praising the Lord and the rest of them kneeled and offered Grace.

"I am sorry for breaking the promise that I had made," sobbed Snow White. "Please forgive me for disobeying you. I……. felt……. sorry for the old lady and ……. I offered her a cup of warm……. water."

"I knew she would be back; we had warned you that she would," Hu muttered glancing at Ha and Dah.

"Who? I didn't get you," asked Snow White puzzled.

The dwarves just stared at her in disbelief.

"I still can't understand how this happened. Did Lady Helen really master the art of disguise or did you place your brain in a jar before opening the door for her, Saphead?" Khaa snarled.

Snow White was stunned and shaken. She started sobbing, "She definitely……. didn't look like ………the Lady…… I am……. sorry for being a……. a dullard."

"Stop crying and never call yourself a dullard, or anything as such," sobbed Wah. "Snow White, your kindness blinded you. It's not your fault."

Snow White pulled her hands out of the covers to wipe her tears. Her eyes suddenly fell on her hands, she gasped in horror and screamed, "GOOD HEAVENS, WHAT…. WHAT HAS HAPPENED TO MY ARMS….AND HANDS…… WHY ARE THEY….SO DARK?"

"It's because of the poison," muttered Dah, "You have got another beautiful colour now, it's ebony or is it inky black? Well, I guess your colour is closer to uhm…… it's…."

"It's raven, isn't it?" giggled Ha.

Snow White yelled, "STOP! STOP IT! WHAT ABOUT…… MY FACE …AND ……AND MY NECK…AND MY …….MY LEGS?" She quickly got up from the cot and checked her legs, they were dark too, she shrieked loudly, "NOOOOO!"

The dwarves were utterly shocked, they stared at Snow White.

"Yes Saphead, your face has also turned into the same dark ebony colour," Khaa said curling his lips furiously.

Snow White wailed bitterly, "I AM RUINED! How shall I ever return to my kingdom? My parents……they ……they shall never recognise me and…….and …. the Prince, he shall NEVER accept me as his bride…. NEVER… NEVER."

Snow White is Heartbroken

"Calm down, calm down, young girl. I cannot understand why you are hysterical, my precious one. You are completely safe from the poison," explained Hu calmly.

"LOOK AT ME! I AM DARK NOW! I LOATHE DARK SKIN! I don't want to look at myself....... I am not Snow White anymore.... I am ugly now.... please do something quickly and help me....... HELP ME GET BACK MY SNOW WHITE SKIN," cried Snow White despairingly.

The dwarves were shocked to see Snow White in such a miserable state. They simply couldn't understand her depressed condition.

Dah and Wah walked towards her in a state of shock and both of them tried to move her hands away from her face.

"Calm down, my beautiful girl. You are the same sweet, kind, beautiful girl....... nothing has changed about you except for your colour, so why do you weep?" asked Wah, looking puzzled.

"Embrace this beautiful change," said Dah., "and you shall see the real beauty hidden inside you."

Snow white pushed their hands and yelled, "NO! NO! I am not beautiful anymore....... I AM NOT WHITE. How can I face my father....... my mother and all the people of my kingdom? I have been admired for my beauty and white skin," Snow White sobbed. "Now....... now they will mock me. Mother......oh, my mother shall not be able to bear this. She had so earnestly prayed for a child with skin as white as snow. I am no more Snow White."

Khaa couldn't control himself, he roared, "WHAT HAS THE COLOUR OF YOUR SKIN GOT TO DO WITH YOUR BEAUTY? OUTRAGEOUS! I can't believe this! This girl is really a dullard."

Snow White glared at Khaa and blasted out, "How do you know about our people? We are not forest beings like you. For us, beauty is all about the colour of our skin and physical appearance."

Hu gave Khaa a sour look before glancing at Snow White, "My apologies, my precious child. We didn't know about the beauty standards in your part of the world." He patted Snow White's head and continued, "For us, every creation, be it black or white, is unique and beautiful in its own way. We believe the Beautiful God created everything beautiful."

Snow White couldn't understand what he said and didn't try delving into it as well. She went on wailing with her hands covering her face.

The dwarves were disappointed. They never expected Snow White, schooled by the best tutors, to be obsessed with her physical appearance.

CHAPTER 27

SNOW WHITE'S MELANCHOLY DAYS

A week had passed since Snow White's colour transformation and she was still in a state of deep melancholy. She felt disgusted and ugly. She did not want to look at her arms and hands. She completely covered herself in a thick blanket and spent her days weeping inside the confines of her bedroom.

The dwarves tried to counsel and change her conditioned perception of beauty, but Snow White was not ready to listen.

"Why are you not ready to believe the truth?" Aah asked, unable to comprehend the pain of Snow White.

"Oh, my dear friend! You are such a mumpsimus, how could you have such an insane perception of beauty?" sighed Dah excitedly. "You shall have to change your perception, what you—"

"Dah, you shall remain silent for some time," said Hu shortly. He glared at Snow White for a while and explained to the rest, "She has been conditioned to believe that everything white is beautiful. It's not her fault, we simply can't change her perception now."

After Hu's explanation, the rest of the dwarves stopped troubling her with their questions.

Back in the castle, Lady Helen was having nightmares of being pushed into a large pit of fire by Madame Quine. She would wake up immediately and rush to the bathroom and cry mercilessly thinking of little Snow white in her arms and all her evil deeds.

One night, she felt different after having accepted her mistake and repented consciously in her prayer just after a similar nightmare. She had fallen asleep just after her repentance and had a dream of the two men she had met in the forest and who had shown her the way to the Princess's hideout. She saw them holding her hands and taking her to the castle arena which had suddenly turned green and bright. She felt blissful that night.

But in the days that followed, she became quiet and aloof. She stopped looking at herself in the mirror as it started reflecting her face as ugly and distorted. She even feared facing the Queen and would try not to come near her.

Lord Ferdinand was worried about his beautiful wife acting strange and hysterical, "My gorgeous Lady, you have to accept the truth and move on. I understand how much you loved her, but she's gone…. we tried our best in searching for her."

These words made Lady Helen even more miserable. How could she ever tell her husband that she is the one responsible for Snow White's disappearance? She had to forever live a life with extreme feelings of shame and guilt. Her consciousness was trying to push the truth from inside her, but the fear of being rejected by her husband and ridiculed by the people stopped her from telling the truth.

CHAPTER 28

PRINCE SOLOMON FINDS SNOW WHITE

Prince Solomon looked at the big, red oak tree and thought to himself, "I am sure Lady Helen must have been mistaken, that girl she saw has to be the Princess."

The flowers were wet and glistening brightly in the morning glory and the Prince saw birds pecking on seeds strewn outside the tree.

"Someone has been busy in the garden?" the Prince said thoughtfully staring at the seeds, "I shall have to find out."

He climbed the hill and looked around. He could hear someone weeping. As he moved closer to that strange weeping sound, he found a red deer cuddled tightly by a strange figure under a Loganberry tree. The strange figure was fully covered in a blanket from head to toe.

"Is that.... you .... Princess Snow White?" cried the Prince.

Snow White suddenly looked up. She was startled to see Prince Solomon right in front of her. "PRINCE ....PRI.... NCE SO......SOLOMON???" she shrieked.

Prince Solomon stared in disbelief. He stared at her eyes, the same icy blue eyes. He didn't want to look at that face any longer. He turned his gaze away.

"My apologies for having addressed you as such," said the Prince nervously. "I …… I was misguided………I mean, deluded by my own beliefs……. I am sorry you are not whom I am looking for," said the Prince miserably. He turned his horse around and started to ride away.

"STOP! Prince Solomon……. STOP! For heaven's sake look at me," Snow White implored. "I AM YOUR PRINCESS SNOW WHITE……PLEASE DON'T GO AWAY."

Prince Solomon was shocked beyond words. The girl's voice was exactly the same as that of the Princess. He peered at Snow White horridly.

"I was poisoned and….and the poison…. turned my skin dark, but….but my dwarf friends have promised me that they ……. shall get the colour transformation herbs very soon and…… and I shall get back my colour," cried Snow White with hopes glimmering in her eyes. "I shall be back home soon after that……. Prince Solomon, I am sure you shall come here to chaperone, won't you, my Prince?" implored Snow White looking into the Prince's eyes.

"I am not your Prince and I do not wish to know your story," said the Prince coldly, "I shall make it quite clear that I DO NOT KNOW ANY PRINCESS SNOW WHITE. Now please excuse me."

He rode away swiftly, ignoring Snow White's heart-wrenching wails and screams from behind.

Snow White fell down and sobbed bitterly.

Prince Solomon Finds Snow White

In the evening, the dwarves returned and did not find Snow White anywhere inside their tree house.

"She's not here as well," cried Wah, searching in the kitchen.

"Stop crying and instead go search outside the tree," instructed Hu, looking worried.

"Let's not waste our time searching for that saphead," Khaa grumbled.

Hu glared at him.

Dah was feeling excited, "Where has this girl gone so late in the evening? Good heavens, how are we ever going to find her? I...... I am sure she is lost. She must have—"

"STOP!" yelled Hu. Everyone froze for a second, ran outside swiftly and climbed the hill behind their tree.

"There she is, my poor girl," sobbed Wah pointing to the Loganberry tree.

Snow White was lying under the tree, crying. Guzza was lying beside her with a sullen face imitating her cry and gestures.

"Pray, what happened, my precious one?" Hu asked, patting her forehead. "Ha, come here and take Guzza inside." Ha couldn't stop giggling seeing Guzza imitate both Snow White and Hu.

"Pri......nce.... Solomon he.... he left me," sobbed Snow White trying to swallow her sobs.

Hu looked at her intensely and took her hand in his and said, "First, let us get back home."

Snow White stopped crying, dabbed her tears and walked with him towards their home. After settling on her bed, she told them everything that had happened early during the day.

"Hmm.... so he never loved you, he only loved the colour of your skin," Aah said thoughtfully.

"Why do you shed tears for that filthy beast?" scowled Khaa.

"But I loved him, my love for him is real," Snow White cried.

"Why did you fall in love with him?" asked Hu. "What's the one thing that moved your heart?"

Snow White went pale, she had no answer.

They left her to think about it herself. She spent the whole night finding out why she had fallen in love with him.

CHAPTER 29

HU'S PROMISE

Snow White spent the rest of the days weeping and cursing her life. She kept thinking about Prince Solomon and his spiteful remarks.

Ha and Wah tried a lot to cheer her up but none of their tactics had any effect on her. The only thing she desperately wanted was the colour transformation herbs.

Every night, as soon as the dwarves would walk in, she would run over to them and ask, "Did you get the herbs?"

This went on for a week and after nearly one long week, on a Sunday evening, Hu went over to her and sat beside her. He gestured the rest of the dwarves to sit as well.

Snow White stood up and looked at everyone hopefully, "Have you got the herbs?"

"Our apologies, young lady, but we didn't. In fact, we have been searching for your herbs everywhere for almost a week," said Dah without taking a breath, "from the very next day you changed colour, we—"

"Dah, enough!" Hu had to stop him as usual. He slowly turned his gaze towards Snow White and said, "My precious one, do not worry. There is a way to get the colour transformation herbs."

"How? From where? Do tell me please," cried Snow White excitedly.

"For that, we shall all have to travel to another world," Hu said, lowering his voice.

"Another world? I didn't quite understand," said Snow White, looking puzzled.

Hu smiled, "Are you ready to travel, my precious one?"

"Yes, most certainly, I am ready," beamed Snow White for the first time after losing her white colour.

CHAPTER 30

THE KINGDOM OF THE WHITES

Snow White climbed the steep hill along with the dwarves. She had put on a balaclava and a big black cloak to cover herself. After getting down the hill, she walked with her friends who were all holding flat drums and flutes. Khaa and Nah were holding sharp axes. The dwarves walked together towards a river a little distance away. It was late afternoon, so the water was shining under the light of the bright sun.

They got on a boat and rowed in the clear, blue, silent waters.

Snow White gazed above and saw a flurry of birds of every kind and colour. They had formed a colourful canopy above. Wah and Aah started playing their flutes to match the songs of the birds. It was as though the birds were leading the dwarves to their abode. The rest of the dwarves were humming a tune matching the flute music.

The boat moored to a valley between the grey Rocky Mountains.

Snow White and the dwarves got down and walked through the valley.

Snow White could hear the twittering and chirping of birds and echoes of distant bellows and howls.

"Let's climb the old mountain there," said Aah pointing to a cliff with a rounded peak.

Ha and Wah helped Snow White climb the steep cliff.

After reaching the summit, Dah pointed to a distant forest and whispered softly, "That's where we work, Nature's Secret Sanctuary. Do you want to know what we do there? Well, we—"

"Dah, you shall stop blabbering," Hu said, peering at Dah.

Snow White sensed Hu's reluctance in discussing their work. She respected his decision and asked nothing about it. But she was curious to know what the sanctuary looked like. She saw a vague outline of a spread of vast blue and green space filled with trees, streams and waterfalls. It was the most beautiful sight she had ever witnessed.

"Splendid!" she sighed.

"Yes, indeed," cried Wah wiping his eyes free of tears.

Ha giggled at Wah, "Your tears are getting wasted here, let's drop them into the river, it shall be of some use there." Snow White laughed with Ha.

"Well, I am proud of my tears," said Wah wiping his tears. He turned to Snow White and sobbed, "My dear friend, whenever you feel emotional allow your tears to flow."

"And do not forget to laugh heartily when you feel joyful and light," giggled Ha.

Snow White nodded at both her friends and holding their hands, she slowly started climbing down the cliff.

After getting down, they walked towards another cliff which wasn't very high. The sun was setting and the sky was getting dark. The dwarves looked up at the sky as if making sure of something.

They slowly looked at each other and suddenly became very quiet. Even the garrulous Dah was silent. Snow White felt strange, they were definitely hiding something from her. They climbed the cliff beating their drums softly; Snow White followed them. Once they reached the summit, Hu told her to sit on the far end of the cliff. He then gestured to Khaa to follow him. The two dwarves made a pyre in the centre. Nah poured oil into it little by little.

Once the pyre was lit, the dwarves formed a large circle and started drumming. They started howling and calling out their names. They were swaying, jumping and whirling. Snow white felt odd seeing the dwarves howl like wolves. As she was intently watching their strange ritual, she sensed someone standing behind her. She slowly turned around and was horrified to see a wolf staring at the dwarves. There were some more on the other side of the cliff and more were padding on. Very soon they had covered the cliff all around. She looked at the dwarves for help, but they were too engrossed in their ritual.

Snow White stood there petrified. She didn't move and didn't dare to look into the wolves' eyes. The dwarves began to howl loudly and the wolves repeated the howls in the same pattern. The dwarves were soon whirling beating their drums and calling out their names loudly and hysterically.

Six hours had passed, and Snow White's legs began to ache. She slowly sat down and looked up at the sky. The moon was rising in the inky black sky. The wolves started howling mercilessly and the dwarves matched up to their sounds by spinning faster. As the moon stationed itself like a big pearl against the dark backdrop, a cool breeze started blowing, making the whole ambience heavenly. Hu and Nah whirled around to the centre. They held their flat drums towards the moon and started banging them loudly. The other dwarves spun for a long time and suddenly stopped. They got covered in a cloud of fog. Slowly the fog drifted away from each one of them. Snow White let out a loud shrill. All the five dwarves except for Hu and Nah had turned into trees.

Hu and Nah looked at all the trees and went to each one of them and bowed. They then closed their eyes and began chanting softly. As soon as they opened their eyes, they walked towards the pyre and took the sharp axes and walked back towards the first tree.

Nah's eyes were blood red and Hu's deep violet. They called out Aah's name and chopped the first tree into half.

"NOOOOOOOO…….STOP……..STOP," screamed Snow White at the top of her voice. But Nah kept chopping it into bits. She couldn't run because of the wolves who were now all around her. They were growling at her. She was frightened and was breathing heavily.

Hu and Nah did their merciless act on all four trees as well after calling out the names of the other dwarves. Snow White covered her mouth and cried, "What has happened to you both? How could you turn so evil?"

After they had chopped all of them, they carried the logs to the burning pyre.

"NOOOOOOO!" screamed Snow White. But it was too late. Hu had already thrown the first bundle of logs into the pyre which soon started to blaze. Snow White could feel the heat on her skin.

The whole pack of wolves started moving towards the pyre. They began howling in a rhythm looking up at the moon. Hu and Nah started chanting continuously all the time going around the pyre.

After a long time, they both knelt on either side of the scorching flames and wailed loudly.

And shortly after, grey clouds started moving towards the centre of the cliff. There was a sudden downpour of rain. The fire in the pyre was put out completely. The clouds moved away revealing the full moon again. The wolves started howling again as if crying. The air on top of the cliff was completely covered with smoke. There was nothing remaining of the five dwarves except their ashes. Snow White also cried with the wolves. She couldn't believe what she had witnessed.

Hu and Nah prostrated on the ground and stopped chanting. The wolves padded even closer towards the pyre and covered that space completely. The two dwarves could not be seen anymore. There was a deep silence.

Snow White got up and went closer towards the centre of the cliff where the wolves had settled. She was not afraid of them anymore. The intense grief had taken over her fear. She tried to find Hu and Nah but couldn't see them. But she could hear a faint sound of both their names echoing around that space. She stood there for a long time and nothing happened. The wolves closed their eyes. Snow White started feeling dizzy because of the smoke around. She moved away at the far end and lay down. She soon fell asleep.

She didn't know for how long she had slept for as soon as she lifted her eyelids, she saw the sky lighted above. Birds were chirping incessantly. "Was it all a dream?" she thought to herself. She turned towards her left and saw the wolves still there. She quickly got up. Seeing her stride towards them, the wolves started moving away, but there were two huge, grey wolves who were standing firmly and howling unceasingly. One had deep violet eyes and the other red.

Once the wolves had all moved away, Snow White gasped in horror, "WHAT – IS – THAT?" she screamed. In place of the huge pyre stood a five-headed wolf with a body of a giant dragon. It had large scythe-shaped wings. All five heads were howling along with the other two huge wolves. Snow White shrieked in horror and started to run behind the pack of wolves. But the two big, grey wolves jumped in front of her and blocked her. Snow White froze.

"Do not fear, my precious one," said the wolf with violet eyes. "I am Hu and the wolf here with me is Nah."

Snow White couldn't believe what she had just heard, she was dumbfounded. Hu pulled her cloak with his teeth and took her towards the five-headed wolf. "These are your other five friends – Aah, Dah, Wah, Ha and Khaa."

Snow White stared at them and sobbed.

"My precious one, do not weep. We may have changed our physical forms, but we remain the same inside," said Hu.

"But…. But why aren't they talking? Why are my friends so quiet?" cried Snow White.

"The five-headed wolf is not supposed to speak," laughed Hu. "I, the seventh one and Nah, the first one has separated from them to guide you. In our flight to the first world, I shall control the head of this beast and Nah shall control the tail. Together we become one great beast—Yijinn."

Snow White looked into each of the wolf head's eyes. Their eyes were orange, yellow, green, blue and indigo.

She turned to Hu and asked, "But you had chopped them all mercilessly, how could you turn so evil? I never thought you both could do such a heinous act."

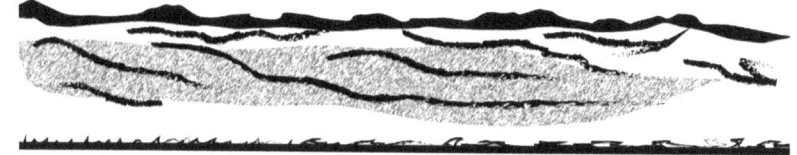

"Truth can sometimes hurt, it can look deceptive at times," said Hu thoughtfully. "That's why I always say do not judge what you see and do not be quick in reacting. There can be a great truth hidden in the evilest of acts. You may now mount the beast after me," said Hu.

He mounted it and helped Snow White mount it. Nah sat on the tail. Snow White was a bit hesitant and had no idea how the ride was going to be. She felt weird talking to two wolves and sitting with them.

"Do not get apprehensive, my precious one. You can hold on to my tail," advised Hu. "Relax and enjoy the flight."

Before Snow White could ask what that meant, Yijinn bolted at high speed and instead of climbing down, it leaped into mid-air. Snow White held Hu's tail tightly and yelled. The beast soared in great speed. Soon the land beneath vanished completely and all they could see were specks of green below.

As they flew higher and higher, the colour of the sky changed into different hues of purple, pink and orange. Snow White felt the cool breeze hit her face.

After journeying for a long time in the air, Yijinn started plummeting towards a white patch of land. Once they had landed on a white-capped mountain, Hu, Nah and Snow White got down. The beast followed the two wolves and Snow White down the mountain.

The pine trees were all covered with snow and so was the ground.

"This is the White Valley where it snows throughout the year," said Hu.

Snow White started to shiver and was finding it difficult to walk, but the wolves were padding with ease. Hu took the beast to a cave in a valley between the mountains.

Hu asked Snow White to wait outside the cave.

Snow White waited outside for a very long time. She was shivering in the cold, "Why is it taking them so long? I shall die of cold now."

Suddenly two tall, white men dressed in long, white robes came out of the cave.

"Who.... who ... are you both?" cried Snow White, looking frightened.

"Do not get puzzled, my friend," smiled Hu. "I am Hu and this is Nah with me."

Snow White stared at them in disbelief, they both had somewhat the same features when looked closely.

"We disguise ourselves according to the requirements of the place so that we may not be suspected," said Hu.

"Did you ever come to my land disguised?" asked Snow White curiously.

"Hmm, my precious one, when you reach your kingdom, you may happen to meet farmers working in the fields, do stop by to greet them," winked Hu.

"Farmers?" said Snow White in a surprised tone. Both Hu and Nah kept quiet.

She felt strange, very strange.

"Take this, my precious child, and cover yourself," said Hu giving Snow White a long woollen shawl.

Snow White covered her face completely and began to walk with them.

"Why can't I too transform myself this way instead of searching for the herbs?" implored Snow White suddenly. "You might as well teach me this magic."

"It is not magic, it's a skill," said Nah quietly.

"It took us years to master this skill and it can be frightening in the beginning," added Hu.

Snow White couldn't understand anything at all. She wanted to ask Hu if they were really dwarves or was that a disguise as well. But she knew Hu wouldn't answer anything now.

"Where are we heading to?" Snow White asked, shivering under the shawl.

"The Crystal Palace," replied Hu moving briskly with Nah by his side.

Finally, after trudging in the snow for a long time, Snow White and the two dwarves reached a beautiful white Crystal Palace which looked as though it was carved from ice.

Through a secret passage, they led Snow White inside an arena. Arrangements were being made for a grand event.

Hu looked at Snow White intently and muttered, "We can get the transformation herbs from the Queen of this kingdom. But for that, you should win her heart. And the only way is for you to participate in the grand event which will be held in a week's time from now."

"But what's the event about?" asked Snow White nervously.

"The Queen is going to crown the most beautiful princess from among the contestants. You have to charm the Queen," replied Hu.

"And win the swordplay contest," added Nah.

"But…… but……. how can I……. participate? I am not skilled in swordplay I…… I…… only know a few elements," cried Snow White.

"Do not get apprehensive, my precious child, follow me," commanded Hu.

He led her outside the arena towards the right end of the palace. They walked on a straight road which was fully covered in snow. After trudging for a while, they reached a fork in the path. From there, they plodded a little further and reached a row of white stone cabins. Hu knocked at the door of the second cabin and waited.

A plum, fair lady in her mid-fifties opened the door and grinned. She was wearing a blue, plain frock and a white bonnet.

"Welcome, Mr. Hugg. Please come in."

"Hugg? So, they are hiding their whole identity," Snow White thought to herself.

The lady squinted at Snow White and muttered, "Hmm, so this must be the girl you had asked me to train, if I am not wrong, Mr. Hugg."

"Yes, this is Snow White and please give her the best training you can," said Hu looking at Snow White affectionately.

"Hello, Miss Snow White, nice to meet you. I am Ava and I shall be training you in the art of swordplay," she stared at Snow White for a while and added, "I presume you would not like to reveal your face right now. I would not want to tamper with your decision. Well, there's very little time so let's get started right away. Oh, good heavens! I mean, from tomorrow morning," she chuckled and led them upstairs.

Snow White entered a cosy bedroom with a low, wooden bed. She went and sat on a wooden armchair in front of the fireplace to warm herself. Her legs were aching badly.

When she was about to get into bed, Hu entered with a tray. He kept the tray with a bowl of hot soup made of root vegetables and a piece of flat bread in front of Snow White.

"I am quite certain that you must be famished after the arduous walk, my precious one?" Hu said with a soft gaze that warmed Snow White's heart.

"Yes, most certainly I am famished," Snow White smiled. She grabbed the tray and gobbled up the soup and the bread in no time.

"Did you just forget to give Grace?" asked Hu.

"Oh, I am sorry, I shall give right away," Snow White said, feeling ashamed.

"There is nothing to feel ashamed about, my precious child," said Hu smiling, "You shall soon find out the power of words, especially the words 'THANK YOU'. You may now go to sleep. Peace."

"Peace," replied Snow White.

The next morning, Snow White woke up to a loud knock at the door. She quickly wore her balaclava and her shawl on top of it and opened the door.

She found Lady Ava standing outside the door smiling, "A very good morning to you, young lady. Please freshen up, you shall have breakfast now. Your first session of swordplay lessons starts sharply at 7 am."

Snow White nodded and ran down to join the two Hu and Nah for breakfast. Immediately after her morning meal, she headed straight to the backyard of the stone house for her first swordplay lesson with Lady Ava.

"Miss Snow White, you may stand quietly for some time," said Lady Ava who was busy cleaning the swords.

"Yes, Lady Ava," said Snow White with a bit of a quiver in her voice.

Lady Ava moved closer to Snow White, lifted the two swords high up in the air and closed her eyes. She started muttering something in a very low voice. With her eyes still closed, she asked Snow White to close her eyes as well and focus on her breath for half an hour.

"Be in the present moment and don't let any frivolous thoughts enter your mind. Imagine yourself as a great fighter and let the sword do the talking," said the lady in a deep voice.

And shortly after, they started the practise. Lady Ava kept reminding her to forget about everyone and everything while fighting. "Tame the beast, young lady. Once he's tamed the game becomes pure magic."

Snow White suddenly reminisced about her days in Cleistra and her practise sessions with her cousins. Her cousin Evelyn used to address her sword as beast, just like Lady Ava. Their motivational words kept ringing in her ears. She felt lighter and started playing better. Lady Ava was impressed.

For the next three days, they practised rigorously until Snow White was confident enough to compete with the best.

CHAPTER 31

THE CROWNING CEREMONY

The arena was packed with people of the White Valley. Snow White could only see the colour white around. Men and women had painted their faces white and even wore white tunics and robes.

The Queen arrived dressed in pure white silk embellished with white pearls. She had white, flawless skin and golden tresses which were adorned with white feathers. Snow White was feeling uneasy in front of all the white people around.

The contestants lined up in two rows. They had all covered their faces like Snow White.

The Queen looked at each one of them, rose from her throne and announced in a clear voice, "All the contestants shall have to combat in two rounds. The contestants who lead in both matches shall go to the third round and compete with each other on beauty, poise and elegance. The winner shall be crowned The Most Beautiful Princess of White Valley.

Snow White was tensed upon hearing the third round. She wasn't aware of the final beauty round. She tried to check for Hu and

Nah but couldn't find them anywhere. She had no other choice but to compete with the rest as she was pushed into the arena first for the first round.

Snow White played the best among all and won both rounds. Tumultuous applause followed after her second win.

All the finalists ran to get themselves groomed and dressed for the final round.

Snow White remained in the arena. The audience was curious to see Snow White more than anyone. The girls came back with white, glowing faces and wearing white, flowing silks.

They went and stood on a golden pedestal each.

"You may all unveil your faces and introduce yourselves," announced the Queen, staring at Snow White.

The girls proudly introduced themselves one by one.

It was now the turn of Snow White. The Queen and her people were waiting anxiously for her to unveil. They expected her to be the fairest and the most beautiful as she was the only one who didn't go to get groomed.

Snow White unveiled and stood in front of the Queen.

"OH MY, GOOD HEAVENS! WHO THE HELL IS SHE?" shrieked the Queen in horror seeing the ebony black Snow White.

People moaned and cursed loudly "A witch! A black witch!".

The rest of the contestants screamed and moved away from her.

"YOU LOATHSOME BLACK WITCH! HOW DARE YOU PARTICIPATE IN THIS EVENT!" growled the Queen, "WHO LET YOU ENTER OUR KINGDOM?"

Snow White stood on the pedestal in front of her trembling, "I…...I am…. Snow White…… Princess Snow White from the Kingdom of Levon. I was fair and beautiful, but because of a ……. a poison……. my skin turned dark."

The Queen yelled at the top of her voice, "What a lie! Guards! Guards! Take that filthy witch away!"

Snow White sobbed loudly and ran towards the arena gates.

Two wolves were waiting outside for her. Snow White immediately recognised them because of the colour of their eyes. They pulled the teary-eyed Snow White swiftly towards the cave where they had hidden the five-headed beast. They helped her mount the beast. After Nah and Hu mounted, they quickly took off from the snow-filled grounds towards the blue skies above.

"Don't lose hope, my precious one. We still got two more places to go," consoled Hu.

CHAPTER 32

THE DARK KINGDOM

After a long tiring flight, the beast landed in a hot desert. Both Hu and Nah looked calm and unruffled even under the scorching sun, but it wasn't the same for Snow White. The sudden change in temperature made her overwhelmed and exhausted. And moreover, she always hated the Sun.

Hu discerned Snow White's discomfort. He gestured Nah to come forward. Nah walked slowly and thoughtfully. He gestured Snow White to kneel. He placed his two paws on her head. Snow White felt the strange vibrations again but this time more intensely.

"My precious child, do not resist the change of patterns around you, be it the temperature inside or outside you, the change in your food, your clothing, the ambience or even the people. Accept them all. Sudden and unimaginable changes come with great lessons, if we accept them and show our gratitude, we shall be taken to a path where a multitude of changes take place inside us, at a faster pace. And our earlier perceptions, that we were so sincerely clinging on to, shall be snatched away from us and destroyed. And at the end of all this, we become renewed and re-energised," explained Hu from behind.

"It's cleansing," whispered Nah.

Snow White didn't understand. She shook her head and sat down, thinking.

Nah stood in front of her on all fours and looked straight into her eyes. His eyes widened and his eyeballs vanished.

Snow White shivered again but was ready to witness the truth that his eyes portrayed.

She saw her reflection in it, she was enclosed in a cage made of innumerable grids as if imprisoned. She looked closely and saw five birds with human baby faces pulling the grids from outside. She could also see three very wild and fiery-eyed women on the other side of the cage trying hard to break the grids. Seven enormous cockroaches were crawling all over her. And a gigantic, powerful eagle with an old woman's wrinkled face was on top of the cage hitting the grids with her huge beak desperately trying to free Snow White.

"Be in the moment and accept the change," said Hu suddenly, "Observe your thoughts and don't try to stop them."

Snow White observed her thoughts. As she did, her thoughts started fading away one by one. For a minute, she managed to be in a thoughtless state. She was dumbstruck. The baby-faced birds, the monstrous-looking women and the mighty eagle broke the grids and pulled her out. She felt her arms, legs, head and torso getting disentangled from each other. She couldn't feel her body, she felt light, very light. She whirled and whirled and started floating in a massive purple expanse of ether. She went through different emotions. At first, she felt cheerful and innocent like a baby, then a gushing sense of fieriness swept across her whole being which was followed by a great sense of power and magnificence. And once all these emotions started spreading out into the vast expanse, she felt lighter. But suddenly, the creepy cockroaches started pulling her to a dark space. It was mysterious and scary but a little whimsical at the same time.

As she was about to fully delve into that dark space, everything inside Nah's eyes vanished. She was back in her body. She felt heavy again.

Nah moved away from her. Snow White was exhausted and dizzy, "What was that?" cried Snow White, looking at Hu. Hu howled and continued to move.

"Was it all a dream?" thought Snow White to herself.

"If you survive a storm, you become wiser," said Hu suddenly. "But you have to accept the storm without resisting it, you shall soon find out. Have patience, my precious one."

Snow White continued walking even though she could not stop thinking about what she had just witnessed in Nah's eyes.

Hu and Nah kept the beast hidden in an underground cave and disguised themselves again, this time into sturdy, black men in long robes and heavy turbans.

Snow white looked at them in surprise and thought to herself, "Do they really have a permanent physical form?" She now even doubted their home inside the oak tree. "Was that just an illusion? Was I hypnotized into believing it?" She shuddered at the weirdness of all her experiences with her dwarf friends. She thought no more, resisted no more but just moved along with them.

"We are heading towards the Dark Kingdom a little further away from here," breathed Hu, looking ahead towards the north.

They reached a red-coloured tent in the middle of the vast desert.

Hu went inside and after a while came out with a hefty, tall man with very dark skin. He was dressed in a long-tattered robe with long sleeves and a colourful turban.

He squinted at Snow White and greeted her and quietly led everyone to a fleet of camels. The camels were basking in the hot sun not bothered about the two strangers gasping at them. Hu and Nah found them amusing.

The tall dark man pointed towards a brown, medium-sized camel.

"My precious one, you may mount on this camel here," said Hu firmly. "We are heading towards the Dark Dome Palace to meet the Queen. It's a long journey from here, you shall get exhausted if you walk."

Snow White mounted the camel's back while Hu and Nah just walked along.

After two hours' tiresome journey, they reached the Dark Dome Palace which was beautifully constructed in the centre of sprawling grounds. The dome was deep red, sitting atop a black, stone, octagonal base.

Hu showed Snow White the palace and soon after gestured her to move outside the palace grounds towards the city. The city was not far away. It was very colourful and bright.

The market was open and lively. Vendors were shouting and yelling from their stalls, calling people to buy their goods. Snow White noticed that the people were all dark-skinned, just like her. She felt one among them now and wasn't afraid to be caught.

They reached the dead end of the city. Hu pointed at an orange, dome-shaped house, "Let's walk towards that house."

After reaching the house, Hu banged at the door instead of knocking. As soon as the door opened, Snow White saw a very tall and sturdy woman with dark smooth skin standing right in front of them. She was wearing a flashy, bright, yellow skirt and bodice with red floral designs.

"Welcome Habbab and Bazem," greeted the lady.

Snow White glared at Hu and Nah suspiciously after hearing their new names.

Hu gave her a quick glance and then turned towards the lady, "Peace, Madam Sheri. This is the young lady I told you about the other day."

Snow White was puzzled at what Hu had just said. "The other day? When was that?" thought she.

The lady smiled warmly and looked fondly at Snow White, "Please come in, young lady. Feel at home." Snow White gazed at her and didn't smile.

The lady slowly walked towards Snow White and hugged her warmly.

The lady sat on the floor mat holding Snow White's hand and spoke softly, "I am Sheri or Madam Sheri, the seamstress as I am popularly known as in this Kingdom. Now young girl, it's time to introduce yourself."

Before Snow White could answer Hu interrupted, "She's Ebony... Ebony Black." He winked at Snow White who was raging with anger.

But she kept quiet seeing the warmth in Madam Sheri's eyes.

"What a beautiful name, dear! Now let me get a few lovely fabrics for you to choose from for your gown," said Madam Sheri cheerfully and trotted towards the stairs.

"How dare you introduce me as Ebony Black?" bellowed Snow White looking coldly at Hu. "Are you mocking me?"

Both Hu and Nah were shocked at Snow White's rude attitude.

Before Hu could clarify, Snow White continued, "Why on earth would I need an outfit from her? Did you see what she was wearing? It's the ugliest-looking outfit I've ever seen. I shall not wear anything that she sews." She stomped out of the seamstress's house in a fury.

Nah prodded behind her.

"Snow White, don't you want to get back your colour?" asked Nah very slowly. "This is all part of the big plan that Hu has devised. Hu knows what he's doing. You have got to trust him and cooperate."

Snow White was quiet for a while. For the first time, Nah had addressed her by her name. She walked inside glum-faced and carefully removed her cloak and veil.

"Bless my soul! I have never seen someone so elegant and beautiful as you before," gasped Madam Sheri. "You have got the most beautiful colour and skin." She stared at Snow White for a while before taking her measurements. She happily pulled out some gaudy fabrics and showed them to her.

Snow White was feeling disgusted seeing the colours and bold prints of the fabrics.

"Look at this one, isn't this gorgeous?" cried Madam Sheri holding a bright pink silk with enormous floral designs. "You shall wear a frock from this one, my gorgeous girl." Snow White said nothing. She was feeling awkward and uneasy hearing praises of her dark skin.

After the seamstress was done with her measurements, they bid her goodbye and headed back to the red tent to visit Mr. Thabo again, but this time for a different reason.

CHAPTER 33

MURRA

Mr. Thabo took them to the same herd of camels in the vast stretch of open desert sands. He looked at Hu and pointed to a large, black dromedary, "This is the best beast I have, Murra."

"My precious one, Mr. Thabo shall train you in camel riding," Hu said slowly to Snow White who was looking very puzzled. "You shall have to show your camel riding skills to Queen Hayat. Once she's impressed, we can get the magic herbs from her."

Snow White had a lot of doubts, she wasn't sure of how she could win the Queen's heart by riding an animal she knew nothing about. Snow White kept quiet and didn't bother to argue as she desperately wanted to get the herbs. With a lot of difficulty, she got on top of the beast.

Mr. Thabo looked at Hu and smiled, "The training begins now!"

CHAPTER 34

SNOW WHITE WINS THE CAMEL RACE

Snow White had perfected the skill of camel riding and was ready for the camel racing event.

She reached the Dark Dome Palace and headed straight to the royal grounds. Queen Hayat sat on a high throne with the other royals of her kingdom sitting all around her in the gallery. The Queen had dark and silky-smooth skin and she was wearing a heavy, bright orange silk gown with long loose sleeves. She had tied a green silk turban around her head with golden leaf motifs.

The skin of everyone in the arena including the contestants was dark and smooth like that of the Queen. Snow White felt she too had become a part of their clan. She wasn't happy about that feeling but she didn't let her emotions affect her mental strength. She had to win this race to get back her colour.

The race began and everyone set off in their camels. Snow White didn't have to whip her camel like the rest of the contestants as Murra knew what she had to do. Snow White was smart enough to have formed a strong bond with Murra in the few days of her training. Her Aunt Catherin's and cousins' words kept ringing in her ears, "Snow White, you are an exceptional rider. You just got to form a stronger bond with your steed." This thought and the desperate urge to get the transformation herbs helped Snow White to finish the race first and emerge as the winner. Queen Hayat was impressed.

CHAPTER 35

THE MOST BEAUTIFUL BLACK PRINCESS

Snow White stood with the rest of the two finalists who secured the second and third positions in the camel racing event. She was dressed in a gaudy pink gown with bright floral designs adorned with gold beading. It had a square neckline and dropped sleeves. She had never worn such a lurid outfit before. She felt strange and wild.

The rest of the two contestants were also dressed in brightly coloured silks with extravagant designs. All three wore turbans with golden butterfly motifs. Each of the contestants had to introduce themselves to the Queen and had to move their body rhythmically to a wild music played by the royal musicians.

"I am Ebony Black. I am strong, beautiful and enigmatic," shouted Snow White loudly. After introducing herself, she performed a wild dance that Madam Sheri had taught her. Though she wasn't very comfortable doing it, she did it with great enthusiasm to impress the Queen.

The Queen smiled as Snow White danced and did her own little dance from the gallery.

Everyone applauded after the grand show. The results were announced and as expected Snow White was crowned as The Most Beautiful Princess. She was invited to the Royal Feast immediately after the commencement of the function.

Snow White stepped inside the Dark Dome Palace. She was awestruck at the beauty inside. A giant candelabrum with innumerable candles hung in the middle of the dome-shaped hallway. The ceiling had beautiful mural paintings in blue and white. There were golden pillars with intricate designs of camels and cats. Snow White couldn't take her eyes off the walls. They were adorned with stone-carved faces of wild men and women.

Snow White saw Queen Hayat strutting towards her. Snow White curtseyed and forced a smile, "Good day, Your Majesty."

"Good day to you as well, Princess Ebony Black," smiled the Queen. "You have got plenty of time left to marvel at the aesthetic beauty of this palace. Now, let's have our meal."

She led Snow White to a large dining area with carved chairs and a long table to match the space. The table was filled with big golden bowls of delicacies.

Snow White offered Grace and then enjoyed the meal even though she didn't actually know what she was eating.

"How lucky for an ordinary girl to have a seat next to the Queen!" whispered the maidservants from behind the table. "Look how she is acting like a real princess."

Snow White bit back a sharp retort. She desperately wanted to tell them that she was a real Princess. Her eyes then suddenly fell on the wall behind the Queen. The Queen caught her sight.

"Your painting shall also find a place there, Princess Ebony. Those are the winners like you," the Queen said proudly. "I am the one in the far end to the right. I was the best camel rider back then.

But after taking up a challenge against Prince Shakh and losing to him, I lost all my confidence. I vowed never to sit on a camel again."

Snow White looked at the Queen's teary eyes.

The Queen got up and walked towards her portrait, "I could have won had I not listened to his words and believed in them. I got frightened and that took away my confidence and strength."

The Queen turned to look at Snow White. She stared at her with her piercing eyes. Snow White felt nervous and gave her an expressive smile.

"I presume it's time for you to retire," said the Queen firmly.

The housekeeper led Snow White to her chamber.

Snow White stepped inside a carpeted anti-chamber that led to a large, dome-shaped room with a huge candelabrum in the centre. There was a beautifully carved canopy bed and a cedar wood dresser lined with crystal bottles filled with musk.

Snow White sat on an oversized red velvet chair and gazed at the burning candles on the candelabrum and thought, "It gives the same light as the candles in my chamber back home."

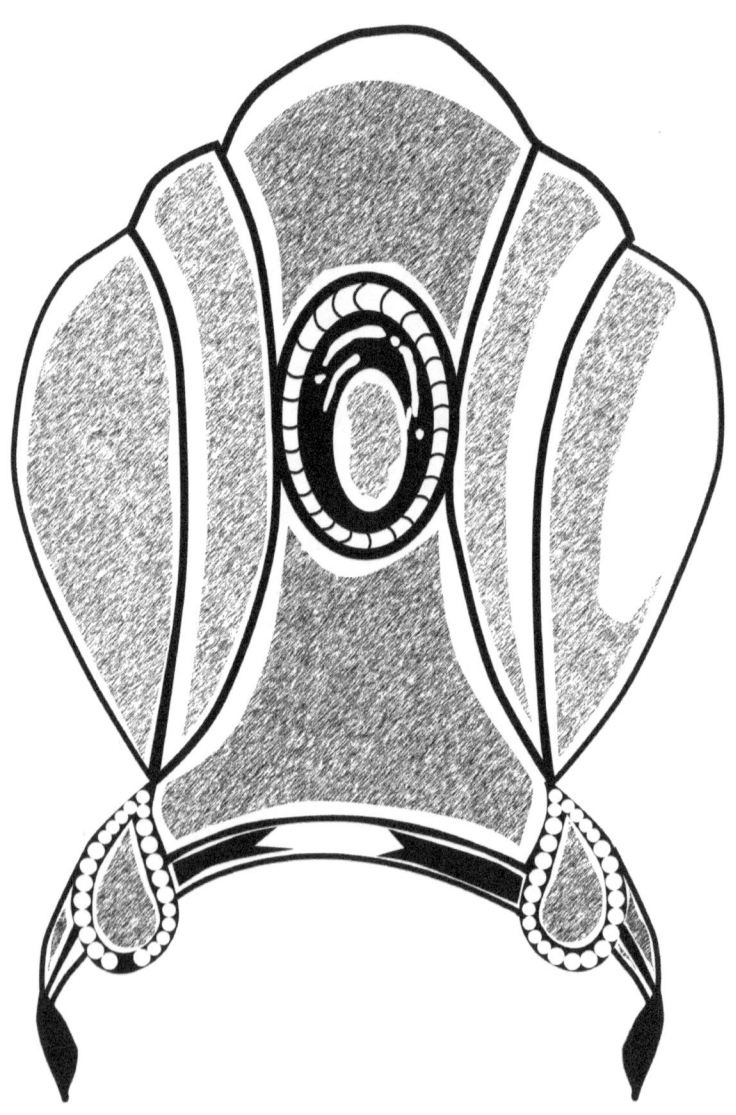

CHAPTER 36

THE OROMO CROWN

Snow White selected the only light-shaded gown from her wardrobe. She looked at herself in the mirror for the first time after her skin had turned dark, "I look like a black princess." She felt different. She had become wild and bold. "Who am I? I cannot find elegance and softness in me anymore. I have lost them."

She recalled her earlier days in her kingdom, the fair-skinned girl who despised dark-skinned people and now here she was, a black girl herself. She smiled at the irony of life.

She was unconsciously introspecting her life and the great changes that affected her when she heard a faint knock on the door; it was Kiara, the housekeeper, "Good morning, Your Highness, the Queen has summoned you down for breakfast."

Snow White gazed at Kiara. She resembled Cora a lot, the same gentle smile and the same gestures. She felt guilty about her behaviour then. She could not repay for the pain she had caused Cora but she could be more mindful of her words and actions now.

"Yes, Kiara, I shall come down for breakfast soon and of course a very good morning to you as well," Snow White said gently. "Kiara, could you please first help me with this turban?"

"Yes, most certainly, Your Highness," smiled Kiara taking the long piece of green silk from Snow White's hand.

Once she was ready with her turban on, she had to muster great courage to look at herself in the mirror. She couldn't see herself in the old, habitual way anymore. But the courage that she mustered and the different way of looking at herself now, gave her an inner strength which was intense.

She suddenly thought about the human-faced eagle she had seen in Nah's eyes, "Is all this a part of that great process?" thought Snow White to herself.

Still lost in thoughts, she slowly strolled towards the dining area in her new attire and a new role.

"A very good morning to you, Your Majesty!" said Snow White very politely.

"Good morning, my beautiful Princess. Are you enjoying your stay here, my child?" the Queen enquired staring at Snow White's turban.

"Yes, Your Majesty," Snow White replied feeling rather heavy under the silk turban.

"What is bothering you, my child?" the Queen asked.

"Nothing at all, Your Majesty! I am perfectly fine," said Snow White, forcing a fake smile.

They soon sat down to have a lavish breakfast. It was a quiet affair. After the meal, the Queen took her to the wall of portraits.

"I always wanted a portrait of mine in the centre of this wall, adorning the Oromo Crown," said the Queen staring at the beautiful portraits on the wall.

"You shall try once more, Your Majesty. I am sure you shall win the crown," Snow White said trying to please the Queen.

The Queen smiled, "You flatter me, my beautiful Princess. But I do not think that is possible now. I do not have enough strength or patience to even try it. I cannot fulfil that dream of mine, but I think *you* can."

"ME?" Snow White asked, looking stunned.

"Yes, you, my brave girl. I saw how you handled that black beast so efficiently, you were far better than how I was back then," said the Queen pointing at her portrait, "and you always know what you are doing. You have got great strength. You just got to believe in your strengths more and not listen to anyone else. I want your portrait right beside mine, *you* wearing the Oromo Crown."

She left Snow White feeling perplexed and nervous.

CHAPTER 37

PRINCE IGOBO

Snow White saw a dark, huge figure of a man riding an equally huge camel approaching her. She kept riding and patting Murra continuously. The man stopped in front of Murra. His brown and gold velvet robe was gleaming brightly in the sunlight.

"Good day, gorgeous lady. I am Prince Igobo from the Kingdom of Burbuz," and with a loud evil chuckle he added, "Do not turn the beast into a pet lest she shall forget her task."

Snow White smirked and continued patting her camel.

"I presume the Queen is pampering you a lot, you being her next pawn," beamed the Prince. "But I am sure you must have heard about my father, the great King Shakh, and his feats from Her Majesty herself."

Snow White kept quiet. Prince Igobo gazed at Snow White, "You are a very beautiful, young woman. But your strength shall never match the son of King Shakh. There's still time to back off. I do not wish to win over a beautiful woman easily."

Snow White looked at him and scowled, "I prize accomplishments over beauty, Your Royal Highness. You shall witness that on the royal grounds soon."

She rode away leaving Prince Igobo fuming with rage.

CHAPTER 38

SNOW WHITE WINS THE OROMO CROWN

The great arena was packed with spectators. They were waiting with panted breath to see Snow White compete with Prince Igobo the Unbeatable. Only the Queen believed in Snow White, everyone else in the kingdom was sure that it would be an easy win for Prince Igobo as always.

The race began and the camels with their riders took off swiftly. Prince Igobo was confident of his win. He didn't have to exert much.

Snow White meanwhile only focused on herself. She didn't even for once look at Prince Igobo. She kept giving her best and Murra knew her strengths as well. Snow White felt bad for Murra, she was pushing her a lot. She patted Murra's neck continuously and kept apologising to her.

While riding, Queen Hayat's words kept echoing in her ears, "There's nothing you cannot accomplish if your belief in acquiring it is strong enough."

Snow White fled with Murra and didn't for once turn back. Murra kept moving confidently. She knew what she was doing. And finally, Murra and her master reached the finishing line.

Snow White realized that she had won the Oromo Crown only when the whole crowd rose and screamed in chorus, "Ebony Black, you did it!" The echoes of the applause and cheers from all around the arena, made her weep.

CHAPTER 39

QUEEN HAYAT'S WISH

The Queen placed Snow White's painted portrait wearing the Oromo Crown next to hers. She took Snow White's hands in hers and looked at her fondly, "I have never been this happy my entire life, Ebony, I mean, Princess Ebony Black. I shall coronate you as a princess officially and you shall reign as queen after my tenure."

Snow White was bewildered, she didn't know what to say. The Queen loved her a lot and she had taught Snow White how to believe in her strengths. She could never have won the race without the Queen. She would forever be indebted to her.

Snow White returned to her chamber and sank into her red velvet chair. She gazed outside and inhaled the air filled with the scent of the blue lilies in the golden vase placed on the table beside her. She introspected her achievements, the swordplay event, and the Oromo camel race. A sudden uncontrollable expression of emotion swelled up inside her whole being. She had never felt that before. She had always been appreciated for her beauty alone, but that wasn't an achievement. Her mother's words made sense to her now, "Real joy is achieved on realizing your true strengths and talents, you shall feel a great sense of happiness when you overcome every hurdle that ultimately leads to a profound growth in you and that my child, is real beauty."

Snow White was suddenly interrupted from her thoughts by a loud knock on her door.

A messenger had brought a scroll. It was a message from Hu.

Snow White quickly ran downstairs towards the gate after reading the message. Hu and Nah were standing outside the palace gates, waiting for her.

CHAPTER 40

THE INSIGHT

"Congratulations, Snow White for your great achievement. We heard people talk about you and your great strengths," Hu was looking very proud.

"Thank you, friends. It's because of you both that I won the race and got the crown," smiled Snow White. "The Queen loves me even more now and she wants to coronate me as a princess."

Hu looked at Snow White intently, "My precious child, do you wish to stay here forever as Princess Ebony Black? I believe everyone accepts you as a beautiful princess here and they love you a lot too," and with a certain bit of hesitancy he added, "and you have got all the luxuries as well."

"NO! I am NOT Ebony Black, I am Snow White. This is not me and …and I do not belong in this kingdom," cried Snow White.

Nah looked at her intensely, "And that soft and pretty Princess Snow White which you think you are…..is also not *you*."

Snow White gasped. She was tongue-tied for a moment and couldn't defend herself. She kept quiet and slowly walked back inside without even bidding Hu and Nah goodbye.

During the latter part of the day, Snow White pondered deeply about what Nah had said.

"Maybe Nah is right," she thought, "I may have been living a life of pretence all these years."

CHAPTER 41

SNOW WHITE DECIDES TO ASK FOR THE COLOUR TRANSFORMATION HERB

The Queen was sitting on her large velvet chair and sipping a hot beverage when Snow White walked in.

"Princess Ebony, my dearest, come and sit with me," said Queen Hayat warmly.

Snow White slowly walked towards the Queen, her hands and legs trembling. With a simmering sense of fear she asked, "Your Majesty, I.... have…... something important to ask."

The Queen looked fondly at Snow White and hugged her, "My beautiful Princess, you shall not tremble in front of me. You are not a stranger anymore. Go on my dear girl, I am ready to part with whatever you ask."

"Your Majesty! I.... I am not Ebony Black, I am ......uhm.... Snow White. Princess Snow White, King Arthur's and Queen Cyprus's only daughter," quivered Snow White. "I was poisoned by a lady named Helen. She had abandoned me in a forest out of mere envy and....... later when she came to know that I was still alive, she.... she ...... poisoned me. The poison changed my white skin into black," Snow White paused for a moment and looked at the Queen who was looking extremely horrified. "I ...I want to return home to my parents....... I....... I want to get back my colour and for that, I need your help, Your Majesty. You have got the colour transformation herbs....... I....... I have come here...... for that."

"Colour transformation herbs? Ridiculous! Is this some kind of a joke?" blasted the Queen.

"No.... No... I...I am telling you the truth," Snow White implored, feeling ashamed of herself.

The Queen looked at her furiously, "Why do you want to change your skin colour to white? I despise the colour white. Here we try to darken our skin and we use herbs for that. You have been blessed with the most beautiful skin, which is the dream of every girl here and you want to turn it white and ugly? Are you mentally deranged?"

"NO! NO!... Your.... Majesty it's....it's just...... that I cannot return to my kingdom like this, I mean for the people of my kingdom, having dark skin is....is ugly," sobbed Snow White bitterly. "Just like how.... how... white skin is for you."

"WHAT?? Dark skin is ugly?" roared the Queen. "So, you mean the people of the Dark Kingdom are all ugly and I, the Queen of this kingdom, the Queen who made you a Princess and loved you like her own, is ugly for you?"

"No, Your Majesty. No, I didn't mean that…I am sorry if I have hurt your feelings. I was…. just trying to—"

"GET OUT OF MY KINGDOM!" the Queen yelled, before Snow White could finish her sentence. "Get OUT! I DESPISE LOOKING AT YOU NOW."

Snow White gasped in fear and ran away sobbing.

Hu and Nah were waiting outside, again as grey wolves. They had the same look when Snow White went crying after being yelled at by the Queen of the White Kingdom. They pulled Snow White's cloak and ran towards the underground cave.

"Nothing is working, I feel I shall never get back my colour," cried Snow White forlornly. She sat on the hot sand and started wailing bitterly.

"There's still hope, come on get up, we have one more world left," said Hu. "And you shall definitely find the herbs there."

The three of them mounted the beast and took off to another world for the third time.

CHAPTER 42

NATURE'S SECRET SANCTUARY

Snow White carefully got down from the beast's back and looked around curiously. It was a barren land. Before Snow White could ask anything, Hu and Nah led the beast to an open ground a little further away. The beast was placed in the middle of the ground which was thick with mire.

Hu and Nah started howling and running around the beast, calling out AAH's name again and again as if exhaling. All five heads growled at the two wolves. The beast ran uncontrollably, he looked furious. Hu and Nah ran behind and jumped on the beast. The beast tried to charge at Hu. Nah ran swiftly and pulled the beast's tail with his teeth. He controlled the beast from behind, Hu jumped on its neck and controlled the heads. They repeated Aah's name. The beast calmed down and started sinking into the wet soil. Hu and Nah looked at the beast and started laughing uncontrollably, "HA…. HA……. HA…… HA."

Snow White looked puzzled. She had never seen Hu and Nah laugh at anyone.

As both the wolves kept laughing and howling, the beast all covered in muck, rose above with the help of a sudden gusty wind.

The five-headed beast started moving up and down vigorously and the whole place was vibrating. The two grey wolves looked at him intensely and began to shout DAH…. DAH…. DAH. The beast dashed above like a thunderbolt and started moving faster in the open endless space and kept flying until both the wolves below roared KHAA…. KHAA…...KHAA very fiercely and loudly. The mighty beast kept dropping down ferociously spitting fiery flames all around. He was now burning in his own flames. Both Hu and Nah stopped for some time watching him burn.

Snow White was horrified. She screamed and yelled at the two wolves to stop the flames, but because of the intense vibrations and heavy wind, she couldn't move. Hu and Nah turned around and began to wail   WAH……. WAH……WAH. They sobbed and wailed loudly, calling out Wah's name. As if the rain gods had heard their cry, the clouds moved from above, the sky turned grey and in no time, there was a downpour of heavy rain. The fire was put off. But the five-headed beast was gone, nothing was left of the mighty beast except for his grey ashes and the thick smoke all around. Snow White was deeply upset. She cried bitterly.

Hu and Nah trod towards the middle of the ground which was completely covered with ashes and smoke. Nah began running here and there howling and inhaling his name NAH …… NAH…… NAH…...Hu started running in circles exhaling HU…… HU…….HU again and again. Suddenly a cool breeze blew and the grey ashes began swirling above like a whirlpool. Out of it, a hexagonal grid emerged. Nah and Hu jumped and turned around calling out the five dwarves' names – AAH, DAH, HA, WAH and KHAA. The hexagons started separating, each time they called out a dwarf's name. The separated hexagons were vibrating and spinning vigorously. After a while, they began clustering together, forming five stars. The stars started spinning and moving all around Hu and Nah.

The vibrations were unbearable and Snow White covered her ears. Her head began to ache because of the intensity of the vibrations. Hu and Nah howled loudly and continuously for a long time. Then they stopped.

The sun emerged from between the clouds and spread its light on all the stars. Snow White was suddenly blinded by the blazing light. She tried hard to peer through it, but she couldn't. An hour had elapsed and still, everything remained the same. But suddenly something incredible happened. The sun moved away and hid behind the clouds. She turned to look at the stars. She was stunned. The five stars were now filled with the seven hues of the rainbow instead of the grey smoke. And the colours were all moving and mixing. And in a few moments from then, each of the stars had only one prominent, prismatic colour left on them and each colour was different from the rest.

Soon after, the colours began to blend with the golden bright borders of each star. Hu and Nah looked at them. They howled for one last time and fell on the muck. They rolled on the dirt all the time calling out all the dwarves' names including theirs as well.

A bright golden light suddenly flashed above. Snow White was completely blinded. She was curious to know what would happen next, so she kept peering through the blinding light. It took some time for the light to become a bit warmer for Snow White to see clearly. Through her half-opened eyes, she saw two enormous golden orbs in the centre of the five auras of bright, white light.

"The stars got probably changed into those five auras," thought Snow White. She was amazed to see birds of different sizes and colours flying towards the sky, just above the open ground. They formed a canopy and started singing their songs. The auras started fading, and from each of the bright auras, the five dwarves— Dah, Aah, Wah, Ha and Khaa stepped out. Hu and Nah stepped out from the golden orbs above. They were all back in their dwarf selves.

Snow white was bewildered at all that she had just witnessed, it was magical. She cried, laughed, jumped and clapped seeing her friends back in their dwarf forms. But none of the dwarves noticed her. They silently sat down in deep contemplation for some time to get back to their selves.

Hu opened his eyes first. He glanced at Snow White who was still gaping in disbelief at what she had just seen.

He went over to her and explained, "The five-headed beast was created by the energies of all those five friends of yours. Their energies had to be combined to make one magnificent creature. The beast had to be fierce to face the gusty winds and fly high and that energy could only be acquired from Khaa. He also had to be light-hearted so as to be tamed and for that we had to combine the energies of both Wah and Ha. He had to be curious and adventurous to find the places we had to visit. The energy of Aah was required to play that part. He had to have the energy of Dah, the unstoppable energy to keep him moving. And with the energies of mine and Nah, we were able to control and lead the beast. Yijinn is the combined energies of all the seven of us."

Snow White was stunned. This was all above her comprehension and understanding.

The five dwarves got up and went over to Snow white. Snow White looked at them with great awe and reverence.

Wah hugged her and sobbed and Ha giggled and laughed.

"Now, let's start moving," said Hu. The dwarves all nodded together. But they weren't walking, they were swaying and hopping. Even Khaa was dancing his way through the ground.

Snow White couldn't control her laughter, "I wonder what just happened to you all. Why are you all dancing instead of walking?"

"That's how we shall be moving from here on," explained Dah.

"But …. but why?" giggled Snow White.

"You shall soon find out," laughed Ha.

They reached a beautiful, green space. It was a utopian world. The floor was carpeted with green moss. The air was cool and filled with the scent of strawberries and pineapples. Numerous trees were coexisting together.

Snow White peered at the trees and everything around. She slowly shifted her gaze towards Dah. Dah smiled and nodded as if reading her mind.

"Isn't this the same place that you showed me from the top of the old mountain before our first journey?" asked Snow White.

Dah nodded, "Yes, this is Nature's Secret Sanctuary and this is the place where we work."

"So, why are we here? We were to travel to the third world, isn't it, Hu?" mumbled Snow White, looking anxiously at Hu.

"This is the third world, my precious child," replied Hu softy.

"And we shall definitely find the transformation herbs here," added Wah and Ha together.

"If you were certain of getting the herbs from here, then why did we have to waste our time visiting the other two worlds?" asked Snow White grimly.

"You shall soon find out the answer to that, my precious one," replied Hu exchanging glances with Nah.

Nah looked at Snow White as if trying to communicate through his silence. Snow White tried to read his mysterious eyes. She could sense something deep, a hidden secret in them. She shuddered and looked away.

Wah and Ha held Snow White's hands and took her deeper inside the sanctuary. Snow White was stunned to see the extent of green space as they went deeper.

They stepped into a beautiful, colourful orchard. Snow White gasped at the sight of the red, shining apples hanging on the trees. Pears, peaches and plums were glistening in the sun. Woodpeckers were pecking on the enormous trees; squirrels were scampering up and down the maple and beech trees and a few hedgehogs were relishing the fallen fruits beneath a cherry tree. The calls of different birds filled the air.

Snow white jumped to pluck a red, juicy apple from an apple tree but was stopped by Aah.

"Snow White, you shall have to first request the tree to let you have one fruit from their branch before plucking one," said Aah.

Snow White was perplexed, she didn't quite understand what Aah had said.

Aah moved towards the tree and touched the bark of the tree gently, "Now, watch me closely." He knelt, closed his eyes, inhaled the fresh air and then exhaled it slowly and whispered, "Peace! My dear apple tree, if you permit, may I have one fruit from your lowest branch?"

To Snow White's astonishment, the tree bowed down. Aah very carefully plucked an apple and handed it to Snow White.

"I wish to communicate with these trees just like you," beamed Snow White with excitement.

"There's nothing to learn in this, it's just your belief," said Hu, patting the trunk of the apple tree. "If you believe they are listening, then you shall see them respond."

Snow White then stared at her red apple for a while, it looked strange to her now. She was about to bite into it when Ha chuckled loudly, "Here you go again! Have you given your prayer of Grace?"

"Why are you always in such haste? Your unmindful eating has still not taught you a lesson," growled Khaa, looking furious.

Snow White turned scarlet from embarrassment. She quickly knelt and prayed.

"You can turn every poison into nectar if you breathe into it the Most Gracious One's name," said Hu firmly.

"I wish you had told me this earlier, the poison wouldn't have changed the colour of my skin," cried Snow White.

"Hu was talking about POISON, you saphead!" bellowed Khaa. Snow White got startled by his words.

Wah ran over to Snow White and pulled her away from Khaa and hugged her. He along with the rest of the dwarves took her to the left side of the orchard into a lush, green landscape. It was covered with plantains, mango trees and short jackfruit trees with enormous fruits hanging low.

Snow White didn't know which space was more beautiful, the orchard that she saw earlier or this tropical space. The dwarves smiled seeing Snow White's reaction.

The stillness of the blue, quiet waters and the coconut trees lined across the riverbank was a sight to behold. Towards the end of the river, elephants, dogs and cows were bathing along with some children. There were others who were enjoying a bath in the burbling waterfall bouncing off the rocks.

Wah and Ha clasped Snow White's hands in theirs and hopped towards the fall, "Let's cleanse ourselves and join their fun."

The children giggled and splashed water on the dwarves. The dwarves splashed back and Snow White did the same. She forgot all her ordeals while drenching and playing in the cool waters. A few naughty chimps jumped into the water and started dancing madly. The children and the dwarves started imitating them. Snow White couldn't stop laughing.

Soon Dah came over and gestured them to come out of the falls.

Snow White and the dwarves ran behind Dah with the chimps and the children following them to a row of marshy fields. Men and women were working together in the beautiful, vast fields. They were singing while doing the chores. Some others were sitting on the ground opposite to the field, weaving mats together. They were singing a different song.

As they walked a little further, they found rows of neatly arranged, thatched shacks surrounded by beautiful green vegetable gardens. "You were right," said Snow White. "Everyone's dancing here instead of walking."

Snow White also saw girls and boys humming a cheery tune and plucking fresh vegetables after taking permission from each plant.

"Why are they plucking just one vegetable from every plant? There are plenty of ripe vegetables on each," muttered Snow White, curious to know more about the weird, happy people of that land.

"Here people work together and share everything they have with each other, even with animals and plants," replied Hu. "They co-exist together and use the resources carefully."

"You shall soon learn the ways of the people here," Aah said slowly.

Suddenly Dah pulled Snow White towards him and away from a tall coconut tree. A big, green, tender coconut landed right in front of her with a thud.

Dah pointed to the girls on top of the tall coconut trees, "Let them finish their job."

When it was safe to cross, the dwarves jumped into the stream one by one and Snow White did the same.

The water was warm. Snow White swam slowly like the rest. Minnows and trout were swimming along with them. They reached the other side of the stream and stepped out into a woodland.

Snow White was feeling exhausted. She had never swum for such a long stretch of time. "Don't you have boats here to cross the stream?"

"We do not use boats here as the waters are sacred," said Aah. "And taking a dip in the waters here can cleanse your whole being."

Snow White held Wah's and Ha's hands and decided to dance like them on the wet, mossy floor of the woodland. Peacocks and peahens were moving fearlessly. They were suddenly disturbed by a race of a herd of red deer.

Snow White gasped in fear seeing a jackal chasing them. "That jackal is so vicious, look at those poor, frightened deer."

"No one's bad or good here. The jackal is playing his part and so are the deer. The jackal's role is to hunt to satisfy his hunger and the deer's role is to escape," muttered Aah. "The deer are always extra cautious, they do not brood over it, they in fact embrace the role that nature has ordained them. And these are all the designs of the great force, isn't it all so strange?"

"And my precious child, understand this lesson carefully. There's always a reason behind the behaviour of someone towards something, no one's good or bad, not even the Lady who poisoned you," Hu advised.

This was a great lesson for Snow White. She kept thinking of this when suddenly she squeaked. Cobras and vipers were slithering across the rustling foliage.

"Don't panic, they shall not hurt unless you provoke them and if perchance you get bitten there are numerous healers in this part of the land," said Dah quickly, "Now, walk along, my friend."

Hu led everyone to a row of mud houses with earthen lamps hanging outside each house.

Snow White was shocked to see men and women wailing loudly, some laughing uncontrollably while many singing and dancing wildly. Wah joined the bawlers and started wailing with them while Ha joined the band of the barrel of laughs. Snow White gasped seeing strong, young men crying like toddlers.

Dah, who was looking thrilled, moved quickly to Snow White and muttered excitedly, "They are expressing themselves. It's all a process of healing."

"We do these all the time here, why do you look so amused?" Aah asked curiously.

"Our men are not supposed to cry or wail, and our women are not supposed to laugh so loud," said Snow White thoughtfully. "I have never seen my father cry."

The dwarves looked at Snow White in amazement except for Hu.

Hu stepped inside the third house on the left side. The others followed him. An elderly woman was sitting and pounding herbs in a pestle, swaying her head from side to side and a boy was lying on a low bamboo cot. Both were singing together.

"With Peace and in the name of the Most Gracious do we enter your humble abode dear Madam Haueffer

With Peace you may welcome our dear friend Snow White who has come for help that only you can offer," sang all the seven dwarves together.

The woman rose and swayed towards Snow White and the dwarves,

"Peace to you my friends from another world,

I welcome the friend of my friends to my abode,

Tell me what help I can offer to this lovely child,

I am always here to serve you with my herbs from the wild."

Snow White started chuckling, seeing everyone sing and dance instead of talking. She started looking at everyone in utter amusement.

"Our dear friend here has lost all joy and vigour because of her lost snow white colour,

We have come to your abode our friend for we are sure with the help of your herbs and hands she shall not have to emotionally suffer," sang Wah and Dah together.

Madam Haueffer looked greatly surprised,

"*I wish I could lend you my eyes that you may see how beautiful you look, my dearest,*

You are unique and you are precious,

I am sure you have never seen your true beauty ever,

For you have just accepted the beauty standards of another."

Wah nodded his head sensing Snow White's uneasiness, he whirled around and cried,

"*O ye great curer of the wounded and the ailing,*

With your magical hands and herbs, please bring back the colour of my dear friend,

for I cannot see her in distress for my heart is greatly aching."

Madam Haueffer hugged Wah and took him by his arm and danced,

"*Do not lament o ye mystical being who weeps in both joy and pain,*

I shall find the herbs for your dear friend, for her desire shall not go in vain."

The dwarves sang the song of goodbye and left Madam Haueffer's shack.

Snow White was still looking amused, she found the ways of the people in the sanctuary weird and funny.

"What is bothering you, my friend?" asked the curious Aah, peering at Snow White.

"You have stopped singing now, why were you all singing while in Madam Haueffer's shack?" asked Snow White.

"That's how people of this part of the world converse, they sing instead of talking and they dance instead of walking. Everything runs on a rhythm here," Dah explained, dancing around with Wah and ha.

"And one more thing, my friend, we adapt ourselves according to the place we are in and the people we are surrounded by," added Aah.

"I believe you do not have a physical form of your own," said Snow White quietly. Dah looked at Hu who gestured not to speak anymore.

Snow White quickly changed the subject, "And what about the snake that bit that boy? Was it venomous? The boy looked so calm and relaxed."

"Yes, it was a venomous one, the black Mamba, the beautiful, black, slithering monster," replied Dah again. "He is a mischievous one."

Snow White gasped, "Bless my soul, did they find the reptile and kill it?"

Ha laughed loudly while Khaa growled.

"If someone from your kin hurts you, do you kill them?" growled Khaa.

"Every creature is part of our big family, my precious one. Some can hurt you as that is the role that they have chosen," said Hu slowly. "Remember, every pain, be it physical, mental or emotional, has a great lesson to convey. So the pain givers, be it a snake or … or even the Lady who tricked you, are there to help you grow." Snow White suddenly became quiet. She kept thinking about Lady Helen.

Hu and the rest of the dwarves took Snow White to a small shack at the far end of the same lane they were in.

"You may stay here, my precious one," said Hu. "We shall all be staying in the shack just preceding this one."

Snow White looked around. There was a low coir stool, an urn and a cup, a mat with a small pillow and a neatly folded blanket.

The dwarves bid Snow White goodbye and left her shack.

Snow White could hear a soft melodious tune coming from outside. She opened her small window and peered. An old man was playing his reed sitting under a mango tree, on the other side of the lane.

"How peaceful and happy they all seem to be!" Snow White thought to herself, "they live such humble lives, yet they are so contend."

She soon drifted to a peaceful and deep slumber on her mat.

CHAPTER 43

THE PROTECTORS OF THE PLANET

Snow White was roused from her deep sleep by the sudden, loud knock on the door. "Good heavens! Who can it be at this hour?"

She very slowly opened the door and found all the seven dwarves outside. "Peace," they said in a chorus.

"What brings you all here? Isn't it terribly early?" asked Snow White, rubbing her eyes.

"Here everyone wakes up before sunrise," said Wah heartily.

"And we expect you to follow the same as long as you are here," scowled Khaa.

"Yes, most certainly, I shall follow every rule of this sanctuary till my very last day here," replied Snow White nervously.

She went inside, hastily changed her robe and set off with the dwarves outside. All the houses had lanterns burning outside. The air was cool and misty. The early birds had started their morning calls with their chirps and tweets.

The dwarves took Snow White to the sacred stream where they all cleansed themselves. Before long, they joined the crowd in the vast, open, green space and prostrated together.

After their group prostration, they sat down with the rest of the people to watch the sunrise. Everybody was silent, only the dawn chorus of robins, chiffchaffs and warblers could be heard. The wait was over. The pale golden sun emerged in all its glory, spreading the vibrant forms of its gold and red hues to the otherwise plain sky.

Snow White witnessed the rising of the magnificent ball of light for the first time. She was also awestruck like the rest of the people around at the sun's magnificence. She had always hated the sun, but now for the first time, she saw beauty in it. The people watched it with the same amazement as her even though they had been witnessing this for years.

They closed their eyes and together thanked the sun with Grace and said a silent prayer. They inhaled the fresh air and, in a chorus, shouted, "We are one."

They all then headed home after hugging and greeting each other. Snow White was bewildered at the whole thing of which she was happy to be a part.

She turned to Wah and Ha, "Do you do this every day here? I haven't seen anyone talk to each other here other than greeting and singing….and the people here are always very calm and happy."

"It's not that everything is perfect here, my precious child, but here people accept the imperfect and treat the struggles and problems as life lessons," explained Hu. "They live in the moment and in harmony with nature and unlike your people, they have not forgotten that they are a part of nature. They do not fear the future and hence do not store food for tomorrow. They treat every living thing with kindness and respect. Did you see anyone sitting on a horse's back or plucking a fruit or a flower without permission?"

Snow white said nothing, she felt a childhood memory emerge from somewhere inside her. It was a question she had asked her mother when she was barely five, and her mother had not replied. Her mother's silence had hurt her then, but if her mother had replied according to her perspective, Snow White could never have understood what Hu had just said.

"Thank you, Mother," whispered Snow White unconsciously. She suddenly turned to look at Nah. She probably had started to comprehend the language of silence and its power. Nah looked at her and smiled.

In the days that followed, Snow White learned the ways of the people of Nature's Secret Sanctuary. She learned how to communicate with plants and animals, learnt the songs of birds, she worked in the fields with everyone and mastered the art of climbing trees. She ate simple meals, started dressing in leaves and stayed in a small shack like the rest of the people.

Madam Haueffer taught her all about herbs and healing. She started spending more time with Nah. She felt a sense of contentment, calmness and peace take over her earlier emotions like fear, anxiety and doubts.

Her perception of Khaa changed as well. She was no more afraid of him; she understood that his fury sprung from the pain he felt for nature. He could always hear the echoes of the cries of the animals and trees being destroyed by humans for their benefit.

One fine morning, during their usual meetups near the stream, Snow White looked at her friends one by one. She could not imagine a life without them now. They had taught her a lot.

"Hu, may I ask you something?" asked Snow White, sounding a little hesitant.

Hu gave a smile of assurance asking her to continue.

"What work do you do here?" asked Snow White.

The dwarves looked at each other and waited for Hu to reply.

"We are the Protectors of the Planet. We, together with the people of this land, conserve the forest by protecting the trees and wildlife," Hu said calmly. "Here you shall find every species of animal and plant, even the ones that are extinct in the rest of the world. We are here to help keep this beautiful planet alive."

Aah suddenly jumped up and started dancing, "When some Earth-loving beings wake up to the call of nature and start a mission to restore the lost forests in their land, we open the doors of this secret sanctuary for them, to help them in their mission."

Snow White looked proudly at the dwarves – the protectors of her planet.

CHAPTER 44

THE RITUAL

Snow White swayed along with the dwarves towards the open pasture near the river. The sky and the Earth below were lit with the dazzling light of the full moon and the flickering lights coming from the rows of lanterns that the people were holding. They were dancing together, silently aware of their position in each row. Snow White and the dwarves joined them with their lanterns.

The whole ambience had a celebratory feeling. A cool breeze wallowed through the air and ruffled Snow White's hair. The sound of crickets and barred owls added to the mystery of the midnight hour.

Snow White was amazed to see the great gathering. Cymbals, tambourines, drums and bells were being played by the children. Men, women and a few other children were dancing to those musical rhythms. Animals were also swaying along with them. Wolves had gathered on top of a distant mountain and were howling in chorus.

Another group of older men and women were stirring broth in a large cauldron. They were uttering some chants and pouring the broth into the coconut shells lined up on the ground.

Once the people had settled down after the dance, children of all sizes and shapes, jumped and hopped towards the cooking fire. They took a bowl each and began serving them to everyone resting after the dance.

They chorused together, "Grace." It was followed by a prayer and they mindfully drank the simple vegetable broth.

Snow White imitated them.

Soon after, Snow White and the dwarves joined the group towards a huge mountain at the far end of the land.

"It is called Mount Mishk," said Dah. "The greater part of this ritual is to climb Mount Mishk and witness the glory of the moon and prostrate together in gratitude."

Snow White was already feeling exhausted. But she kept moving with the rest without complaining.

"Do mindful dancing and breathing, my precious child. You shall not feel tired if you are mindful," Hu advised sensing Snow White's struggle.

"Be the observer," said Nah slowly.

Snow White didn't understand what he said. Dah ran over to Snow White, gleaming with excitement.

"Nah speaks in metaphors. Now let me explain it to you, my friend," said Dah excitedly. "Be aware of your thoughts and do not shun them, for if you do, they start weaving thought after thought. This chain of thoughts shall make you apprehensive and can even mislead you."

"Thank you, Dah. I think now it is quite clear to me," smiled Snow White.

They reached the mountain and started climbing the peak together, holding lanterns and singing the glory of God.

After reaching the summit, they witnessed the moon with all its glory, closed their eyes and sat still taking in the light, beauty and serenity of the moon inside them.

After the first ritual, each took turns to enter a small cave on top of the same mountain. They prostrated and prayed. Everyone waited patiently for their turns.

As soon as they reached the foot of the mountain, they danced wildly and sang all the way back to their homes.

"Shall we also head back to our homes now?" asked Snow White, feeling exhausted.

Ha giggled loudly.

"What's so funny about that?" Snow White looked irritated.

"The ritual isn't over yet. All these men and women shall spend the rest of the early hours in deep contemplation and after that, they shall fast for the next 3 days to feed their souls directly with pure energy," Ha explained giggling.

"Contemplation and fasting?" asked Snow White, puzzled.

Hu held Snow White's hand, "Come with me, my precious one, I shall show you what it's all about."

They hopped towards the same lane where they stayed. Hu and Nah led Snow White to the first shack on the right side of the lane. The others waited outside.

As they stepped inside the small shack, Snow White saw a middle-aged lady sitting cross-legged on the floor with sage burning alongside a clay lantern that was throwing huge shadows all around the walls with its flickering light.

There were three wreaths made of three different kinds of leaves placed in front of her. She was silently breathing with closed eyes. After a while, she took the wreath made of eucalyptus leaves and placed it on her head.

"We shall visit the next house," whispered Hu softly and soon after they reached the second shack where a young man was doing the same ritual alone.

In the third house at the end of the lane to the left, a man and a woman were performing the ritual sitting at the far ends of their room.

"Look Snow White, she got the Holly Oak," hushed Hu softly.

"What is Holly Oak?" Snow White was bemused, "I didn't quite understand this ritual. What are they doing and what do those wreaths signify?"

"They are introspecting their life from the last full moon night to this night," said Hu.

Soon after, he led Snow White outside the third shack, "Each wreath symbolises the steps you have covered in life, to show how much you have grown and in what stage you are. The final wreath is the Holly Oak. If you have realized the light within, in all its glory and have become one with it, then you are entitled to wear it. It may take years for you to wear the Holly Oak. Here you are your own judge, no one sits to judge you. Unlike the events you had seen in the other two worlds and in yours as well, here people compete with their own selves, not with any other. It's personal and you do not let anyone know about your growth. You have to keep working to achieve the wreath of Holly Oak."

"But even if you shall get it after many years," added Aah suddenly, "you shall not stop this ritual. It's a continuous, inner work."

"Once you wear the Holly Oak," said Dah, "your responsibilities towards yourself and the nature around and that includes your people, shall increase."

"But there will come a time in your life when you shall not need the Holly Oak to remind you where you have reached in life," murmured Nah very softly.

"And when shall that be?" asked Snow White.

"When you have nothing to ask for," replied Hu.

"When there's nothing to be afraid of," smiled Dah.

Wah looked at Snow White and sobbed, "When the inner voice and you have become one, and no outside forces affect or bother you."

"When you have accepted yourself completely," said Aah.

"When you have completely realized your strengths," roared Khaa.

"When you realize the beauty within and without," grinned Ha.

Nah looked into Snow White's eyes and breathed, "When the observer and observed become One."

Snow White sat down silently rewinding all that she had heard. She had to unlearn everything she had learned to understand what the dwarves had just said.

She looked at Hu, "But here everyone's perfect, so why do they need to perform this ritual?"

"We all are His creations, my precious one," said Hu. "None are perfect except Him. We are beings with a consciousness that has to be tamed and taught."

Snow White understood. She asked no further.

CHAPTER 45

SNOW WHITE'S SELF-TRANSFORMATION

It had been five months since Snow White started staying in Nature's Secret Sanctuary. She was now a part of the sanctuary. She had slowly started realizing the true meaning of beauty and life. The dwarves would visit her occasionally in the early hours of the day and by afternoon they would return home.

"Peace, my dear friend. I have good news for you today," cried Wah running towards Snow White early during the day.

"Peace," said Snow White waving at her dwarf friends. Khaa was scowling and was in a very bad mood.

"What's wrong? Why is Khaa looking so angry and why are you giggling so loudly, Ha?" asked Snow White.

"Madam Haueffer wants to meet you at once. Come on, let's go," Dah pulled Snow White's right arm.

Snow White did not have time to ask them what it was about. She ran with her friends towards Madam Haueffer's shack.

Madam Haueffer was standing outside her shack holding a bunch of herbs in her hand.

"Come inside my abode, my sweet girl,

With joy and happiness, you may dance and twirl,

For there is something truly amazing that I would like to share,

I have got the herbs that shall help you get back the thing that you deeply desire and crave."

Snow White said nothing. She looked at the dwarves and then at Madam Haueffer. There wasn't any excitement on her face.

Madam Haueffer looked at Snow White and sang,

"What happened my child, aren't you elated?

You do not seem to be happy for the spark in your eyes has just faded."

Snow White was not getting the right words to speak. Hu looked at her as if reading her mind and nodded with a look of assurance in his eyes.

Snow white walked over to Madam Haueffer and hugged her warmly,

"Thank you, Madam Haueffer, for your love and affection,

I am deeply touched and do not know how to express my gratitude and admiration,

I no longer wish to change my colour for I now see beauty in all the colours and even in my own reflection,

I apologise for being blind about my own beauty for my perception was conditioned,

I have finally woken up from my deep slumber and now I am ready to meet my family without any apprehension."

Hu wasn't surprised at all seeing the great change in Snow White. He looked as if he had expected it.

The dwarves looked at each other and smiled, even the ever-furious Khaa had a faint smile on his face. They were not at all surprised at Snow White's great transformation. They had yet again succeeded in their plan, succeeded in preserving the spirit of Nature.

Madam Haueffer hugged Snow White and kissed her softly on her forehead,

"I am proud of you, my dear child, you have grown wise just in time,

Yes, you have to face your people and help them evolve,

For no one is born with a blind soul, they are all conditioned by beliefs that have to be dissolved."

CHAPTER 46

SNOW WHITE GOES BACK TO HER KINGDOM

Snow White knew the secret entry to the castle. She waited till midnight behind the bushes in her backyard. When the whole castle was dark and quiet, she slowly crept inside through a secret, underground passage. She reached the servants' quarters. She had to wait for Martha, whom she believed would help her reach her mother's chamber secretly. She hid behind a huge pillar in the passageway.

Exactly at 3 am, she heard the sound of Martha's footsteps. She peeped from behind the pillar to make sure it was her. Martha was walking silently when Snow White caught her hand. Before she could scream, Snow White stopped her, "NO! please don't, Martha. For heaven's sake!"

"God forbid, who are you?" asked Martha staring at the covered figure.

"I am Snow White, Martha. Please believe me. Come with me," implored Snow White. Martha was stunned. The girl sounded just like the Princess. She quickly followed the girl.

Snow White took her to the attic at the end of the passageway. She unveiled herself and looked straight into Martha's eyes. Martha was dumbfounded. The eyes were the same, but they had softness in them now. The lips were the same, but the smile was genuine now, her breath had the same smell but it was slower now.

"No, this can't be the proud and arrogant Princess who had a strong sense of vanity," thought Martha to herself.

"No, you cannot be Princess Snow White. My Princess would never have the courage to lead a life of a woman of colour. And….and she would never wear anything like this, never," cried Martha.

Snow White hugged Martha, "Yes, I am not that same Princess, I have evolved. I have realized who I am, and what true beauty is. When I took this new form and accepted it fully, I understood what mother and you had always tried to explain."

Martha felt the same warmth in Snow White's hug. Martha recollected how little Snow White would hug her whenever she wanted to explain something. And this time, after many years, she did that again.

"Bless my soul!" sobbed Martha, "You definitely are my Princess. But how….how did this ………. happen?" She kept kissing Snow White and crying uncontrollably.

"I shall tell you everything but not now. First take me to my mother, Martha," pleaded Snow White.

"Yes, Your Royal Highness, I shall take you there. But do not let anyone other than your mother know about your presence," cried Martha. "And my sweet Princess, do not worry about anything, everything shall be alright." She couldn't control her tears.

"Don't worry about me, Martha, I am perfectly alright. I am only worried about mother," said Snow White quietly.

"Your Royal Highness, I cannot believe it's my same Princess who used to be haughty and arrogant. You have indeed evolved into a gracious one," cried Martha, "and you shall not worry about your mother, I shall take care of her."

Martha took Snow White very discreetly to the kitchen and fetched a jug of water, "Your Royal Highness, I shall use this jug of water to get you inside your mother's chamber."

Snow White and Martha had to pass by the guards. The guards never questioned Martha so it was easy for her to take the Princess to the Queen's chamber.

Martha silently opened the doors and placed the jug of water on the Queen's bedside table. The Queen was sound asleep. She was looking weak and tired. Tears rolled down Snow White's cheeks. She kissed her mother's feet softly and very slowly slipped away towards her mother's huge wardrobe.

She looked at the wardrobe and chuckled, "Martha dear, there's enough room for me to lie down and rest here." Martha couldn't bear to see the Princess hiding in her own mother's wardrobe. Her heart ached terribly. She left the chamber crying softly. Snow White quietly adjusted herself to lie down inside the wardrobe and very soon she fell asleep.

Snow White woke up early to the morning calls of the birds. She waited for her mother to wake up. The Queen woke up early as usual and sat on her bed for some time and prayed. She then got up and walked towards her bathroom. After freshening up, she came back and sat on her armchair closing her eyes again in prayer.

Suddenly she felt a pair of soft hands on her shoulder. She opened her eyes frantically and let out a loud shriek, "BLESS MY SOUL! WHO THE HELL ARE YOU AND WHAT ARE YOU DOING IN MY CHAMBER?"

Snow white quickly knelt and whispered, "Shshsh! Mother, quiet! Don't scream! Please for heaven's sake, I am Snow White, your daughter."

"NO! NO! YOU CANNOT BE MY DAUGHTER!" yelled the Queen. "She……my daughter's skin was white …… you can never claim to be my beautiful daughter, GET OUT OF HERE!"

Martha who was waiting outside the Queen's door quickly stepped in. "Your Royal Highness, this girl here is indeed our Princess. Please calm down and listen to her." The Queen was flabbergasted. She covered her face and started sobbing bitterly.

"Look at me, Mother! Look at my eyes, my nose, can't you recognise your daughter's voice? Can't you feel her touch? Is the colour of my skin the only thing that defines me? Mother! Please… please look at me," Snow White moved her mother's hands away from her face and kissed them softly. "Mother! Listen to me, please. I…. I was poisoned and…………. the poison changed the colour of my skin."

Queen Cyprus shrieked, "NO…….NO……NO, this cannot be true."

"Mother, please, don't panic. I am perfectly fine. First, listen to the whole story."

She narrated the whole story of getting trapped in the Dwarf Forest, about Lady Helen leaving her there alone, how she was rescued by the dwarves, the poison apple, and she also gave a brief picture of the three worlds.

Both the Queen and Martha were shocked, shocked beyond words. Teary-eyed, the Queen stared at her daughter and studied her features. Though reluctant at first, she slowly held her daughter's face in her palms and cried, "No, No, this cannot be true. My darling child, how could this happen to you?" She touched her daughter's hair, sobbing. Her once-gorgeous daughter looked more like a forest dweller than a Princess now.

"LADY HELEN! YOU WRETCHED LADY, HOW COULD YOU DO THIS TO MY BEAUTIFUL DAUGHTER? I SHALL NOT SPARE YOU," the Queen cried. She sprang up from her chair and ran towards the door.

Snow White and Martha ran behind her. Snow White stopped her mother from opening the door. She fell on her mother's feet and begged, "Mother, I am still beautiful, if only you could see. Please, Mother, don't tarnish your soul. Don't go out and react. Have mercy on the Lady, pity her for her blindness. She must be suffering with guilt already."

Queen Cyprus was thunderstruck seeing her daughter's unruffled attitude. She looked at Martha for support.

"Your Royal Highness, please let our Princess decide. I believe she has already planned everything," said Martha, admiring Snow White's assertiveness.

"Mother, she didn't poison me but in fact helped me to open my eyes to see the real beauty within and the true meaning of life," Snow White said proudly. "Can't you see how your once proud, arrogant and beauty-obsessed daughter who never ever bothered to talk to you gently has turned into a gentle, simple and happy girl?"

The Queen kissed her daughter and wept, "I love you, my precious one, I missed you a lot. There wasn't a day that I hadn't prayed for your safe return. I knew you were alive and I was certain that one day you shall return to the kingdom. But not like this, my daughter, not like this."

"I know, Mother. It's because of your hope and prayers that I am still alive," whispered Snow White softly. "Mother, if you love me dearly, you shall not disclose the truth of my transformation to anyone, not even to my father. He cannot run this kingdom without his friend Lord Ferdinand. I presume, you very well understood what I meant. Mother, I am very happy and ...... and I am not afraid of people's mockery because I love and respect myself and ......and I do not need validation from anyone."

The Queen cried thinking of how the people of her kingdom would react. She was feeling helpless. Nothing made sense to her now. She just couldn't accept her daughter in dark skin. She cried for a long time. A plethora of emotions floated across her face.

"Instead of thanking God for saving my daughter, I'm sitting and crying, oh how ungrateful of me," wept the Queen. "Thank you, Lord for giving back my daughter."

She hugged her daughter tightly and pleaded, "My dear daughter, go back to the sanctuary and take the herbs from that lady. Please, for your mother's sake. I beg you, I dearly miss your snow-white skin."

"No, Mother. I cannot and shall not do that, that's against my consciousness. I am sorry, Mother. I understand how difficult it must be for you to accept me like this.... but I am sure one day you shall accept me just the way I am now," cried Snow White. "My dear mother, now please go and call father, I cannot wait to meet him."

The Queen wiped her tears, carefully opened her chamber door and quietly stepped outside. Martha followed her.

"Martha, make sure no one enters the chamber except you," instructed the Queen.

Martha nodded, "Most certainly, Your Royal Highness. I shall make sure of that."

Martha left the Queen's hand and walked briskly towards the kitchen. The maids were all lined up for the morning chores, "Dearies, Her Royal Highness the Queen has instructed everyone not to enter her chamber without her permission. Therefore, you shall all abide by this instruction strictly."

"Pray what has befallen our Queen? Hope she is not planning something disgraceful for the kingdom," cried the cook.

"Good heavens, hope she has not murdered the Lady," squealed Lady Helen's maid. Everyone laughed except Martha.

The Queen meanwhile sat down beside the King inside the locked chamber and holding his hands she cried, "My Lord, I have something very important to tell you."

"What's wrong, Your Grace? Are you alright? Tell me what happened." asked the King in a tense voice.

"My Lord, our precious…….. daughter Snow White…… is alive and……. and she's here ………. in my chamber," sobbed the Queen.

The King was startled. He rose from his chair. He couldn't believe what he heard. He bolted towards the door.

"My Lord, STOP! First listen to what I have to tell you," said the Queen in a trembling voice. "You shall not panic seeing her. My Lord……. Our daughter……. Our precious and beautiful daughter has…. Has become dark." She altered the real incident of the poisoned apple and narrated a faked version of the same.

The King was in a terrible shock. He could not fully believe his wife. For a moment, he thought the Queen might have lost her senses as everything sounded so untrue but he nevertheless joined her towards her chamber to clear his doubts.

The Queen looked around and slowly opened her chamber door to let her husband in. After getting in, she quickly locked the door.

She softly called out to Snow White, "Snow White, my precious one, your father is here."

Snow White stepped out from her mother's wardrobe.

The King gasped in disbelief, he felt dizzy and weak on his knees. There, right in front of him was his precious daughter, the only heir to his throne, dressed as a forest dweller with very dark skin.

Snow White ran to her father and hugged him., "My dear Father, I missed you immensely."

The King couldn't believe what he had seen. He cried for the first time ever. But he couldn't kiss her. He simply couldn't accept his daughter in dark skin.

Snow White understood her father's predicament. She left her grip on him and wept, "I shall not face the people of this kingdom until you both accept me wholeheartedly."

CHAPTER 47

SNOW WHITE TURNS EBONY BLACK

Snow White finally managed to convince her parents to accept her just the way she was. Her parents found it really hard to believe their daughter's transformation—from a self-obsessed girl to a genuine and satisfied young lady, who was now not interested in dressing up in the best silk and had no appetite for a lavish meal.

She told her parents about the three worlds she had visited, the lessons she learnt, the medicinal benefits of different herbs, the magic of prayer and the happiness in living in the moment. They would listen to her stories in delight and even though they still wished to see their daughter in white skin, they were very proud of her achievements.

It was now time to reveal to their subjects about their daughter's return. Snow White had spent days in a hideout in her mother's chamber. No one apart from the King, Queen and Martha knew about Snow White's return.

The people were all asked to gather in the arena for a big announcement. Lady Helen came with the other royals and sat beside her husband in the Royal Gallery. The Queen clenched her fists, she wanted to scream out to everyone in the arena about what the Lady had done to her daughter. She stopped herself, for she suddenly remembered the promise she had given her daughter. But she couldn't stop herself from glaring coldly at the Lady. The Lady noticed her glare, she felt miserable. She turned to look away from the Queen.

The whole arena was packed with men, women and children eagerly waiting for the announcement.

With a heavy heart, the King rose from his chair and gently announced, "My dear people, I have an important announcement to make. By the Grace and Mercy of our Lord, our beloved daughter Snow White is ……. alive!"

The Royals, the servants, the guards and the people were all STUNNED.

 Lady Helen's heart sank. She couldn't move, her heart started palpitating and she suddenly started sweating profusely. "No! this cannot be true," she said to herself.

For a moment there was silence.

Then there was a sudden outburst of emotions all around. The royals suppressed their emotions and maintained their etiquettes lest they be ridiculed. But the people gathered in the arena, couldn't control themselves. They squealed, screamed and rejoiced, "Glory to God! Glory to God! Long live our Princess!"

The Queen looked at Lady Helen who was gasping in horror. She sprang up from her chair and was about to leave, when the Queen quickly walked over and gestured her to sit down. Soon after, the Queen went inside to get Snow White. Martha also followed her. And they both returned with Snow White by their side. The Queen's heart was pounding, Martha held her hand tightly to calm her.

Snow White now stood in the gallery facing the people. The royals and the people gasped in disbelief. Lady Helen covered her face with her palms and started sobbing bitterly. She was trembling with fear and guilt. Lord Ferdinand rose from his chair and went to console the King who was looking very disturbed.

"Are you sure, Your Majesty? Is that...... really our Princess?" asked the Lord with a look of uncertainty on his face.

"Yes, she certainly is my precious daughter," replied the King in a quavering voice.

"But how.......... I mean, who did this? My apologies, Your Majesty, but I cannot simply accept the fact that *she* is our beautiful Princess," said the Lord miserably. He suddenly caught sight of the Queen glaring at him. She desperately wanted him to know that his gorgeous wife was the culprit, but when Snow White looked at her, she stopped herself from exploding.

"Have the King and Queen lost their mind?" whispered some.

"Have they thought of adopting this girl and coronating her as our Princess? Who is she? We shall never accept her as our Princess," hushed some others among the crowd. Their whispers echoed everywhere.

The maids and guards were giggling and whispering in pairs. They were waiting for Martha to come down. "Now we know why the Queen had kept us away from the chamber. She was hiding this slave, our Queen has definitely lost her mind."

The King forced a smile at everyone around and said, "This is our daughter and ….and she……."

"Sorry, Father. May I have the permission to continue from here?" Snow White asked calmly. The King nodded at his daughter. He tried hard to conceal his pain but he couldn't. Tears trickled down his cheeks.

The people hushed and whispered. Their Princess sounded the same. But they still couldn't believe their ears.

Lady Helen looked at Snow White and felt a sudden, throbbing pain sweep inside her.

She faced her people and smiled, "I am your Princess Snow White and ...."

There was a sudden silence in the crowd again. Everyone was gasping at Snow White.

"I know I cannot be called Snow White anymore," chuckled Snow White. "You may call me Ebony Black, Princess Ebony Black. You may address me by whatever name you wish to. It doesn't matter to me. What's in a name?" Snow White turned to look at her mother who was swallowing her tears. She quickly trotted towards her mother and hugged her warmly, "Mother, you may cry loudly, please don't hold up your tears."

The Queen kissed her daughter on her forehead, "I am perfectly fine, my dearest. You shall continue speaking."

Snow White turned to look at the people again, "I am no longer your fair and beauty obsessed Princess. I lost my colour because of a poison given to me."

The royals and the subjects were equally thunderstruck. They couldn't hide their expressions. They started whispering and murmuring to each other.

The Queen peered at Lady Helen, who had covered her face with her hands, she was crying uncontrollably. Snow White could also see the Lady crying.

"My dear people, it had been a poison for me then, but now I do not consider it as a poison," said Snow White looking at the Lady. "I do not cry over the loss nor do I think of my past, in fact, I got life's greatest treasure because of this minuscule loss. I have learned things unimaginable and I have even mastered a lot of skills. But the most important thing I got from this unfortunate happening, as you all may call it, is that I have started to accept and love myself just the way I am, I feel more beautiful than ever before. I do not care what others think of me even if they happen to be my own parents, for all that I care about now is to reach my highest self. I have come here to share some of these life lessons with you all because now I truly understand each one of you. I understand and appreciate the work you do and I respect you all for taking up different roles in life, each of you weaving a small part, embracing it wholeheartedly, giving it your best and making this great, dream web called Earth complete."

Lady Helen looked at Snow White and couldn't believe what she just heard, "Is this the same young lady who despised the colour black once?"

The King sat motionless trying to hide his emotions. Queen Cyprus and every single person in the crowd was weeping.

Soon after her speech, Snow White slowly walked towards Lady Helen. Lady Helen froze. She couldn't meet Snow White's eyes, she felt very miserable and guilty. Snow White looked into her eyes for some time and hugged her warmly. She whispered very softly in her ears, "I have already forgiven you, please do not repent. I, in fact want to thank you for showing me my true self, my true strengths and my true beauty. Thank you, my friend."

Queen Cyprus wept silently listening to what her daughter had just whispered to Lady Helen. She felt ashamed of her petty thoughts. Her young daughter had just taught her a great lesson.

CHAPTER 48

EBONY BLACK AND THE PEOPLE OF LEVON

The people of the kingdom couldn't accept Ebony Black as their princess. They prayed and hoped for their Princess to get back her white skin.

The royals on the other hand felt miserable while greeting the dark-skinned Princess. They found it difficult to address her as a princess. Even the guards and servants found it extremely difficult to curtesy and some even mocked her from behind. Snow White knew all about it, but nothing affected her. She accepted the change in their attitude graciously.

Lady Helen stopped getting out of her chamber and spend her days repenting and crying. She couldn't forgive herself for all that she had done. Snow White tried talking to her to get her out of her guilt, but every time she talked, the distraught Lady felt even more guilty. She simply couldn't forgive herself. Snow White eventually had to stop visiting her as the Lady was getting extremely distressed facing her. Snow White instead started sending Martha to console the Lady and ease her pain. And in due course, Martha and the Lady became close friends. Lady Helen felt comfortable in Martha's company.

Months passed by. Snow White was missing her dwarf friends and the people of Nature's Secret Sanctuary immensely. One day she decided to visit them all. She sneaked out of the castle at midnight after informing Martha.

While strolling alone towards the Forbidden Forest she recollected her ride to the forest with Lady Helen. She had got very exhausted that day and here she was now enjoying her stroll and that too barefooted.

She couldn't wait to perform the morning ritual with her friends in the sanctuary. She trod the forest grounds softly so as not to harm any slithering reptiles or wake up any animals. She was no more afraid of the echoes of the distant howls and growls.

She could see the dwarves' home now, the beautiful red oak tree. She danced her way towards the tree, singing softly. But when she got closer, she felt something strange. She looked at the trunk; the bark was completely covered with moss and lichens. She couldn't find the secret opening space that led to the door. She knocked on all the sides of the trunk, but there was no movement. She tried again and again but no one showed up. She looked at the garden outside and couldn't recognise it for it was completely covered with weeds.

Snow White looked behind the tree and saw something strange. There was a huge apple tree with red apples hanging on every branch. Snow White thought for a while and then something suddenly struck her. She remembered how Wah, Aah and Dah had gifted her an apple seed for her love of apples and how they had helped her plant the seed in that same spot where the tree was standing now. The talkative Dah had elaborately explained that it would take around ten whole years for the seed to grow into a tree. Aah had told her that the tree was a gift from her side to the forest and they had even named the tree Snow.

Snow White wasn't amazed anymore at seeing a full-grown tree there in just seventeen months. She had experienced a lot of mysterious events with the dwarves and this was just another one. She wouldn't be surprised if the concept of time and space were completely different there in the forest.

She touched the trunk of the tree and asked, "May I pluck a fruit from the lowest branch of your tree?" The tree bowed and Snow White plucked an apple for her mother. She decided to walk back to the forest edge to get back home. Suddenly she thought of Guzza. She climbed the hill and called out to her pet. No one answered. She ambled towards the end of the hill and looked below. She saw a few wolves chasing a big, red deer. She ran down to see it. The deer spotted Snow White and ran towards her.

"Guzza, is that you?" asked Snow White curiously. The deer didn't reply but kept staring at Snow White. Snow White giggled like Ha and the deer repeated it.

"Oh, Guzza! It's you, you have grown so big." Before Snow White could touch it a big wolf came running and growled at Snow White. Snow White looked into its eyes; they were yellow. The wolf stared at Snow White for a while, tears filled up its deep yellow eyes. It growled again and joined a few other wolves who were hiding behind a thicket of trees. She could see their eyes glimmering in the dark, it was like a rainbow in a dark, night sky. Tears rolled down her cheeks. The wolves howled together in a chorus and slowly padded away along with Guzza.

CHAPTER 49

QUEEN EBONY BLACK

Forty years had passed. Queen Ebony Black got up from her bamboo cot and said her wake-up prayer of gratitude, "Thank you God for another beautiful day". She then stepped out of her little shack and walked with her people to witness the glory of the rising sun. They cleansed themselves in the lake, and prostrated together to perform the prayer. After greeting each other by saying "Peace" they watched the sunrise and offered their gratitude.

Queen Ebony took mindful steps towards the natural reserve. She did not in any way match a royal queen in her appearance. She was dressed in a plain, white cotton gown and was walking barefoot as she always did. She greeted the trees and animals and even checked if they needed something. She smiled at the beautiful spread of green. Her dream of turning the arena into a natural reserve had been fulfilled.

She gazed at the squirrels scurrying up the trees where the chimps had just woken up. Woodpeckers were pecking at the barks of the same tree, annoying the little chimps. Ravens and willow warbles had started their morning calls and the red junglefowls, black bucks and brown bears were moving together silently on the green pastures. Snow White was no more afraid of the venomous snakes slithering by. She was the Master Healer of her kingdom.

She walked further and reached the castle gates. She looked at the castle from afar and smiled at the huge signboard that read, 'Levon School of Life Studies'. She entered the castle. A few children were sitting together cross-legged on the floor, pounding herbs.

"Harry, show me your leg. Do not get frightened little one," said Evelyn, smudging a green paste on a rabbit's leg.

"How is he, Evelyn?" asked Snow White, softly stroking the rabbit's back.

"He is a lot better now," smiled Evelyn.

"Where's Emma?" asked Snow White looking around.

"She's cleaning the kitchen with Eliza and her troupe," grinned Evelyn.

"Alright, I shall join them there," Snow White smiled.

Before heading to the kitchen, she went to the movement and music room. It was the biggest classroom which once was her father's chamber. She joined a small group of children and danced with them. And from there she sprinted towards the kitchen.

"Emma, my dearest, pass me the broom," said Snow White cheerfully. She soon started cleaning the kitchen with Emma and a group of young girls and boys.

"It's sparkling clean now," Emma said cheerfully. "Well done dearies, now we shall all head downstairs to the garden with our Queen." Emma clasped Snow White's hand and gave a soft peck on it.

Tears trickled down Snow White's cheeks. She could not forget the day when Emma and Evelyn had rushed to her side as soon as they heard about her colour transformation. They had embraced her without any hesitation and stood firmly by her side. They

were her pillars of strength. Her dear Aunt Catherine along with Martha had helped her mother accept her dark-skinned daughter completely. She was ever grateful to them.

"I love you, Emma," breathed Snow White and hugged her sister tightly.

Emma ambled along with Snow White while the rest of the girls and boys headed to the pottery class.

"Oh, sister, look at Mark over there, how cheerful he looks!" beamed Emma pointing to a little curly-haired boy playing in the sand with his friends. Boys and girls of all colours and age groups were playing together with their little toys in the sand. There were a few others who were engrossed in painting and clay work. "Cora would have been very happy to see her little grandson."

"Yes, indeed, Emma. I wish she was here to see this," said Snow White staring at the boy, "Isn't he looking adorable?"

Evelyn came running and caught Snow White from behind.

"My dearest sister, you shall come with me now," squealed Evelyn, pulling Snow White's arm.

"Evelyn, when are you going to grow up?" growled Emma.

"I shall start on the same day as you," sniggered Evelyn.

"Good heavens, you both shall never stop your brawls," Snow White laughed. "Now where do you want to take me, my little, naughty sister?"

"My team and I are going to bake a madeleine cake," muttered Evelyn proudly, "and we want you to see how we do it."

"I shall remind you, my annoying little sister that she had already seen you bake that last week. Now leave Snow White alone," scolded Emma.

"Alright, alright, don't quarrel, my lovely sisters," chuckled Snow White. "Evelyn, I shall spend a few minutes with Susan here in the garden and head straight into the kitchen."

Evelyn beamed and sprinted into the castle cheerfully.

Snow White and Emma ran towards the garden giggling to meet Susan. Susan was sitting with a group of small boys and girls, teaching them all about tomatoes.

"Bless my soul! Susan, those tomatoes are sparkling under the morning light," cried Snow White. "We shall have some fresh tomato soup for lunch."

Susan smiled softly, "Yes, most certainly, Your Majesty."

"Oh, my dearest, how many times have I asked you to stop addressing me as Your Majesty? You can call me Ebony or Snow White" giggled Snow White, pinching Susan's cheeks.

"Good heavens, I shall not call you in such a disrespectful manner. Mother had always advised me that whatever happens, I shall always respect you in both words and actions, for you are her queen's precious one," said Susan in a deep voice.

Snow White kissed Susan on her cheeks and said, "I am sure Martha and mother are still together watching over us."

She got up slowly, and proudly looked at everything around her.

Things had changed tremendously in the kingdom. There were no grand events or balls. Butlers, servants and guards were not needed for the castle work. There were no royals or men of rank, everyone worked together and lived in harmony with nature. They were taught responsibility and adherence to the laws of nature. They believed nothing lives for itself – like the Sun they had to spread their light for the world around them.

CHAPTER 50

QUEEN EBONY BLACK WEARS THE WREATH OF HOLLY OAK

Queen Ebony Black sat cross-legged in front of the burning sage and lantern. She inhaled and exhaled slowly and contemplated her life from the last full moon night until the night before, when the moon was back in its full glory.

And after a long stretch of time of sitting in absolute stillness, she opened her eyes very slowly. With folded hands, she whispered the prayer of gratitude. She took the wreath made of Holly Oak and placed it on her head. She had finally worn the Wreath of Self-Realization for the first time ever. She thanked and praised the Lord for a long time and placed the wreath back in her basket.

She rose to her feet with a single effortless movement and walked slowly towards the door carrying her lantern. She kept the door open for the light to seep through. A little chiff chaff sneaked inside and started chanting his chiff chaffs.

"Peace, my little friend, where is the rest of your friends?" As soon as Snow White said this, a flock of chiff chaffs came flying and started singing in chorus. Snow White thanked them for their soothing song. She hopped nimbly singing along with them. Emma, Evelyn and Susan soon joined her morning fun.

After the usual morning rituals, they all strolled together hand in hand towards the castle for their breakfast. Snow White looked at the meal in gratitude—a slice of flat bread and tossed salad served on a banyan tree leaf and a vegetable broth served in a coconut shell.

She closed her eyes and whispered "Grace" and offered the silent prayer, *"Oh Gracious One! I embrace my existence and the role You have ordained for me, for I believe myself to be a part of this beautiful whole...... I am ever thankful to You for bestowing Your great abundance through Mother Nature.... In Thy Presence and in Thy name, I take permission from Mother Nature to let me consume what she has offered me now.... I promise to give back the energy I receive from consuming this portion of her resources to preserve and protect her....Amen."*

The story doesn't end here. It has to continue as there are no full stops in our lives. Hope this tale has inspired you to rethink about your purpose here on earth. If it did, then it's your turn to share your story.

"MAY PEACE AND BLESSINGS BE UPON US ALL"

– **Queen Ebony Black**

www.ingramcontent.com/pod-product-compliance
Lightning Source LLC
LaVergne TN
LVHW041931070526
838199LV00051BA/2775